THE GECKO & STICKY
THE GREATEST POWER

WENDELIN VAN DRAANEN

THE GECKO & STICKY
THE GREATEST POWER

ILLUSTRATED BY
STEPHEN GILPIN

ALFRED A. KNOPF · NEW YORK

THIS IS A BORZOI BOOK PUBLISHED BY ALFRED A. KNOPF

Visit us on the Web! www.randomhouse.com/kids

Educators and librarians, for a variety of teaching tools, visit us at
www.randomhouse.com/teachers

Library of Congress Cataloging-in-Publication Data
Van Draanen, Wendelin.
The Gecko and Sticky : the greatest power / by Wendelin Van Draanen ;
illustrations by Stephen Gilpin. — 1st ed.
p. cm. — (The Gecko and Sticky)
Summary: When the diabolical Damien Black robs a bank and steals a tiger-eye of great sentimental value, he is pursued by thirteen-year-old Dave Sanchez and his sidekick, a talking gecko named Sticky, who are armed with a magical Aztec wristband.
ISBN 978-0-375-84377-8 (trade) — ISBN 978-0-375-94568-7 (lib. bdg.) —
ISBN 978-0-375-85382-1 (e-book)
[1. Bank robberies—Fiction. 2. Adventure and adventurers—Fiction. 3. Magic—Fiction.
4. Geckos—Fiction. 5. Lizards—Fiction. 6. Hispanic Americans—Fiction.]
I. Gilpin, Stephen, ill. II. Title. III. Title: Greatest power.
PZ7.V2745Gec 2009
[Fic]—dc22
2008049794

Printed in the United States of America
May 2009
10 9 8 7 6 5 4 3 2 1

First Edition

For the superhero educators in Bakersfield and Lamont,

and for the kids there who reach for the power inside.

You are *asombrrrrroso*!

CONTENTS

Chapter 1
A WICKED STICK-'EM-UP

"On the floor, all of you!" the masked man snarled as he fanned a gun back and forth across the crowded bank lobby.

At first, people just stared. From his stocking-squooshed face to his gloves to his pointy-booted feet, the bank robber was dressed in all black, with odd whatsits and doodads and peculiar thingama-jigs dangling from a wide black tool belt.

He was a tall man.

A wiry man.

And the gun he held was so strange—a multi-muzzled, peculiar puzzle of a gun.

"NOW!" he screeched at the people in the bank lobby. "Get down or I shoot!"

It may have been a multi-muzzled, peculiar puzzle of a gun, but it was also a try-to-run-and-you'll-be-one-dead-donkey sort of weapon. So with squeals and cries and disbelieving gasps, everyone inside the bank dropped to the floor.

THUMP!

CRASH!

(Jingle-jangle.)

THWOP!

And as they lay there trembling, they all peeked up at the man and wondered the same thing.

Who was this villain, and what sort of wicked, diabolical device *was* that?

The "who" part we will get to in a minute.

The "what" part comes first.

To begin with, the wicked, diabolical device was not a traditional gun that shot traditional bullets through a traditional muzzle.

There was, in fact, very little traditional about it.

The handle was a long canister of highly compressed air, and the gun had twelve barrels fanned out in a semi-circular pattern. One simple pull of the trigger would propel five sleep darts through each opening, immediately dispensing (as you may have already calculated) *sixty* oversized sleep-inducing needles.

Not that any of the trembling, peeking people sprawled out on the bank-lobby floor cared *how* this deadly-looking gun worked—they only wished that the man with the tool belt of dangling doodads would not point it at *them*.

(A foolish thing to wish, as the gun pointed every which way, all at once.)

They also hoped that the villainous man wouldn't come toward them, which, in fact, he did not. Instead, he shouted, "Don't move a muscle!" and darted behind the teller counter, where three clerks had already hit their emergency buttons (to absolutely no avail, as the man with the diabolical dart gun had already deactivated the alarms with one of his mysterious tool-belt doodads).

"Empty the drawers!" he snarled at the tellers, and produced a black sack of strangely stretchy fabric.

The clerks quivered.

And shivered.

And in the end, they delivered.

Stack after stack of cash was shoved into the strangely stretchy sack. And with each stack, the masked man became more and more agitated.

Amped up.

Wired.

"Hurry up!" he commanded. "Quit stalling!"

And then, just as the final drawer was being emptied, he saw something red move on the other side of the counter.

"I said DON'T MOVE!" he screeched, catapulting himself onto the counter so that he could wield his gun to and fro, here and there, back and forth, across both sides of the counter. And he would almost certainly have fled the scene right then if a large ring hadn't caught his eye.

The ring was on the index finger of a woman lying on the floor beside a boy who had a backpack strapped on over a bright red sweatshirt.

It was a tiger-eye ring.

A large one.

With elaborately scrolled gold holding the tiger-eye firmly to the band.

Now, by tiger-eye, I do not mean the actual eye of a tiger.

The actual eye of a tiger would be squishy and slippery and, in a word, gross.

By tiger-eye, I mean a stone that looks (should you have a good imagination) like the eye of a tiger. This particular tiger-eye was honey-colored, with a long slice of black running vertically up the middle, and it looked very much like the eye of a tiger.

Now, a tiger-eye is no diamond. It doesn't glitter or shimmer or refract rays of light. Even when just polished, the stone is, at best, barely shiny. And this particular tiger-eye, although impressive in size, was old and clouded and in dire need of cleaning.

But the squooshy-faced bandit happened to have a weak spot for tiger-eyes.

Especially honey-hued ones with deep black stripes down the middle.

He collected them.

He *treasured* them.

He had, in fact, gone on tiger-eye safaris in Africa, Australia, and (quite foolishly) Arizona but had never seen a specimen as large as the one on this woman's finger.

And so it was that although the squooshy-faced bandit had a sack full of cold, hard cash and should have been making a quick getaway, he instead leapt from the counter, wrestled the ring from the woman's finger, and leapt back onto the counter.

"Stay down, all of you!" he shouted as he added the ring to the sack. And then, although everyone in the bank followed his command, he fired off his multi-muzzled dart gun anyway.

Fwoooosh! Darts shot through the bank lobby.

Clack, he twisted the compression chamber, reloading the gun, and *fwoooosh!* Darts shot the tellers and bank manager (who had come out of his office) and loan officers (who'd been cowering by their desks).

And as he reached the end of his dash along the counter, *clack, fwoooosh!* he shot a third batch of darts behind him for good measure.

Before he'd even slipped through the door, everyone in the bank was deeply asleep.

Chapter 2
LIGHTS OUT

I did say we'd get to the "who" part, and I did promise you "in a minute."

I was, I'm afraid, being overly optimistic.

The fact is, I really should tell you about two other "whos" before I tell you about the bank-robber "who."

The two other "whos" are the boy in the red sweatshirt and the lady with the ring. But there's actually *another* other "who." A "who" I'm quite hesitant to tell you about because you'll likely not believe a word I say after I do (even though it's all genuine, bona fide, documented truth).

So let's start with the boy-in-the-sweatshirt "who," shall we? His name is Dave Sanchez, and the minute the squooshy-faced bank robber opened his mouth, Dave knew exactly who it was.

"That's Damien Black!" he gasped. "He's out of jail?"

And from inside his red ROADRUNNER EXPRESS sweatshirt came a sleepy little voice, "Huh?" followed by the sound of stretching, and then, "Ay-ay. I just had a baaaad dream, *señor*. In my dream, you said Damien Black was out of—"

"Shhh!" Dave whispered.

Suddenly the lady with the ring lurched toward Dave and pulled him to the floor. "Get *down*," she whispered. "And stay quiet! This man is serious!"

Dave was dying to say "Serious? Ms. Kulee, he's *demented*!" but it was at that very moment that the demented Damien Black shouted, "Don't move a muscle!"

So Dave lay still, his brain racing, trying to come up with a way to stop him.

And why, you ask, would a thirteen-year-old boy think he was any match for a demented, diabolical, dart-wielding devil of a man?

The answer is not a simple one.

And it involves that third other "who."

You see, at that moment, a little face peeked out from inside Dave's sweatshirt.

A little gecko face.

One with sharp eyes.

Spotted skin.

And a spicy, snappy tongue.

"Holy guaca-tacarole!" the lizard gasped when he saw Damien Black. "It's him!"

Now, just because *you've* never met a talking gecko lizard doesn't mean a talking gecko lizard doesn't exist. Sticky is, I concede, an anomaly. A one of a kind. A strange twist of nature.

Or, if you must, a freak.

But the fact is, *Sticky* is.

The other fact is that Sticky had forbidden

Dave from telling anyone else that he could talk. It was top-secret. Hush-hush. A keep-it-to-yourself-or-lose-everything sort of situation.

It was plenty bad enough that Damien Black knew.

Still. Sticky had a hard time keeping quiet. "*Ay caramba!*" he murmured from his sneak-a-peek spot inside Dave's sweatshirt. "What are we going to do?"

"Shhhh!" Dave whispered into his shirt. Then, very softly, he said, "I'm thinking Invisibility."

"It won't protect you from the sleep darts," Sticky warned. Having once been a prisoner of Damien Black, Sticky knew exactly what was loaded in the weapon that Damien was holding.

"It won't?" Dave whispered.

"Ay-ay-ay," Sticky grumbled, and although "Ay-ay-ay" can mean many different things when it's coming from the lips of a talking gecko lizard, in this case it was short for Hopping *habañeros, hombre.* Aren't you *ever* going to learn?

11

"Oh yeah," Dave murmured. "People can't *see* me, but I'm still there."

"Correctomundo," Sticky replied.

"But my only other choice is Wall-Walker! That won't do any good. He'll see me and shoot me!"

"Stop talking to yourself!" Ms. Kulee hissed. Then, in an effort to sound reassuring (when she was, in fact, totally stressed out), she whispered, "Everything'll be all right. Just keep still."

But Dave did not want to keep still. He wanted to *do* something. And the reason that he felt that he, at thirteen, could be any match at all for a diabolical man with a multi-muzzled dart gun was because hidden on his arm, under his shirt, under his sweatshirt, was an ancient Aztec wristband.

An ancient Aztec wristband (also known as a powerband) that was (as you may already suspect) magic. Because this powerband had originally been worn by an Aztec warrior, it was much too big for Dave's wrist, so Dave instead wore it on his upper arm.

With the powerband, either Dave could become invisible *or* he could walk on walls. All he had to do was click in a special power ingot ("power ingot" being a fancy way of saying strange-looking, very shiny notched coin). And although there were power ingots besides Wall-Walker and Invisibility, these were the two that Dave had in his possession.

Damien Black, I'm sorry to report, had the others.

So as you see, Damien Black had a history with Dave and Sticky. And with Damien's robbery occurring at the same time Dave was picking up Roadrunner Express delivery envelopes from Ms. Kulee, that history was about to become longer (and, I'm afraid, more convoluted).

"I've got to do *something*," Dave whispered to Sticky.

Sticky tapped his little gecko chin. "As much as I hate to say it," he muttered, "Invisibility would be better than Gecko Power." (Gecko Power being, in Stickynese, the same as Wall-Walker.)

That was all Dave needed. But as he moved to pull the Invisibility ingot from his pocket, Damien Black catapulted up on the teller counter and screeched, "I said DON'T MOVE!"

An eerie silence ensued, followed by a frightening THUNK. And then, from the corner of his eye, Dave could see that Damien was making a dastardly beeline for him.

Dave's heart raced.

His ears filled with pumping blood.

Had Damien recognized him?

Had he heard Sticky's voice?

Would he strip him of his wristband and power ingots?

But as Dave's forehead fired off maddeningly useless sweat bullets, the stocking-faced robber yanked the tiger-eye ring off Ms. Kulee's finger and then, lickety-split, he was back up on the counter, shouting and running and shooting off his multi-muzzled dart gun.

Then, like shutters closing out the light, Dave's eyelids drooped.

They dropped.

And before you could say "Holy tacarole!" Dave Sanchez was fast asleep.

Chapter 3
A BIG, DIABOLICAL BOO-BOO

There was one person who did not get hit by a sleep dart.

Correction.

One *lizard*.

"*Ay caramba!*" Sticky said when all was quiet and he'd emerged from Dave's sweatshirt to a sea of sleeping people.

Ay caramba, indeed.

Despite some behaviors that might lead one to conclude the contrary, Sticky is a good gecko. So the first thing he did was run, lickety-split, to the window, where he saw the last wobblings of a manhole cover clang into place in the middle of a side street.

"Creeping creosote," he muttered, for he knew that the police would not be able to trace Damien Black's footsteps. (Or, even if they could, they certainly wouldn't.)

He had escaped, you see, into the inky, stinky sewer system.

So Sticky zipped back to Dave (who was having a most wonderful dream about flying through the air after a terrified Damien Black, swooping down on the villain, and recovering the bank's cash and Ms. Kulee's ring).

In reality, however, Dave was sacked out on the floor of a bank sawing logs. In fact, he began snoring so loudly that it sounded like he was sawing logs with a full-throttled chain saw.

Then Ms. Kulee revved up *her* sleep saw.

As did the customers.

And the tellers.

And the manager.

The bank was suddenly a cacophonous cavern

of full-throttle snoring. "Ay-ay-ay!" Sticky cried (which, in this case, meant Somebody shut them up!).

Of course the only somebody around was Sticky, so one by one (starting with Dave), he began pulling out sleep darts. And by the time he'd made it back to where he'd started, Dave was waking up.

"Huh?" Dave said groggily. He rubbed an eye and looked inside his sweatshirt. "Sticky?"

"Right here, *hombre*," Sticky whispered, then scampered up his arm and onto his shoulder. "That *loco* honcho got away."

Just then, Ms. Kulee began to move.

Or, more precisely, she *jolted*.

"My ring!" she cried, grabbing the finger where the ring had been. "I can't believe he stole my ring!"

Having something, *anything*, snatched from you is plenty upsetting enough. But when that something is a family heirloom, passed from a great-aunt to a beloved niece, over to a sister, down to a daughter, and on to *her* daughter; when the stone itself was unearthed by that great- (and, yes, often eccentric) aunt on a trek through the wilds of what is now Tanzania (which is, in case you're not familiar, on the eastern side of Africa, below the equator); the stone, the *ring*, becomes more than a clouded tiger-eye in dire need of cleaning.

It becomes a family treasure.

A stony legend.

A compact repository of tall tales and family folklore.

"Why not that woman's diamond bracelet?" Ms. Kulee asked through tears as she looked around the room. "Why not *that* woman's ring? He'll get nothing for mine, but it's priceless to me!"

Now, it was unfortunate for Damien Black that he had pulled his bank heist at a time when Dave was picking up delivery packages from Ms. Kulee.

It was also unfortunate for Damien Black that he did not stick to a straight cash transaction. Money may be valuable (it is, after all, money), but there is nothing sentimental about it.

Jewelry, now that's a different story.

And of all the sentimental diamonds and expensive dangling doodads in the bank that day, Damien Black snatched the most sentimental of all. And he took it from the person who'd given Dave his first job; the person who'd been kind and helpful and had told Dave "Go for it!" when he'd started Roadrunner Express; the person who'd helped Dave build his business to include customers besides City Bank and told him over and over "Keep this up, Mr. Sanchez, and you'll be rich!"

Yes, stealing the money was one thing.

Stealing the ring was quite another.

It was, as Damien would soon discover, a mistake.

An ugly oops.

A big, diabolical boo-boo.

When the police arrived, Dave *tried* to direct them to Damien Black, but the questioning became too invasive.

Too hard to answer.

Too, how do you say, *nosy*.

"Why do you think it was him?"

"How do you know this man?"

"Are you saying you've been to his mansion?"

"How do you know he has a 'thing' for tiger-eyes?"

But the final (and nosiest) question of all was "What's your name, son?"

It was then that Dave realized this was not the best way for him to help. He couldn't risk giving away that he wore an ancient Aztec wristband with mysterious magical powers. He couldn't risk giving away that he'd battled Damien Black in the past . . . and won. He couldn't risk anyone finding out that *he* was the person people in the city had

seen scale sheer walls of tall buildings. He couldn't risk the policemen realizing that *he* was the person they called the Gecko.

So he answered the policemen with a shy "Uh, never mind" and slipped away the first chance he got.

"So, *señor*," Sticky said when they were safely outside. "Are you ready?"

"Ready?" Dave asked, looking at the gecko's expectant face.

"You have walls to walk, *señor*. Bad guys to catch." Sticky climbed fully out of the sweatshirt and perched on Dave's shoulder. "Can't you feel it?" He tugged on Dave's ear, leading him down the street to the manhole cover. "It's time for you to be the Gecko!"

Chapter 4
THE INKY, STINKY SEWER SYSTEM

Dave found a quiet place to take off his red sweatshirt and put on a dark cap and sunglasses. Then he clicked the Invisibility ingot into the Aztec wristband and, *poof*, he disappeared.

"Now where?" he whispered to Sticky. "To the mansion?"

"*Sí, señor*," Sticky whispered back.

"But . . . how? I can't ride my bike . . . and it's a long way!"

"Shhh!" Sticky warned as people were passing by. "Leave the bike. We're taking a zippier way in."

Now, you may be wondering why two completely invisible beings would have to whisper, and the answer is quite simple.

Being invisible does not make your *voice* invisible.

Or, rather, it does not make your voice in*audible*.

And hearing voices that are coming from nowhere frightens people. It makes them think they're in the midst of ghosts.

Spirits.

Poltergeists that will walk through their walls and shake their chandeliers.

Evil entities that will frighten them with chilling gusts of wind and eerie moaning and groaning and *woooooooo*ing in the night.

It is definitely wise to be, *shhhhhh*, very quiet when you're invisible.

And, you may also be wondering, if Dave, *and* his clothes, *and* the backpack he carried, *and* the talking lizard on his shoulder all became invisible, then why wouldn't his *bike* become invisible, too, should he hop on it and ride?

Unfortunately, the explanation is not a simple one. It has to do with particle cancellation and ion phasing and a mysterious rearrangement of the visibility spectrum.

In other words, the science behind the magic of invisibility is not entirely understood. It's a little like electricity. It works the way it does, and we just accept that and get on with things.

What Dave was getting on with at that moment was wrestling back the manhole cover in the middle of the street. "Why am I doing this?" he whispered.

"*Ándale, hombre!*" Sticky urged. "People are coming!"

A manhole cover is a heavy thing, and Dave could not help but moan and groan as he scraped it back, and Sticky could not help but tell him, "Shhhh! Shhhhh!"

To the people on the street, it looked as though someone was moving the cover from *beneath* it. So when all that emerged from the opening in the street were intermittent wisps of steam, the moaning and groaning and *shhhhh*ing sounds took on an eerie feel. A ghastly, ghostly feel. A better-run-for-your-life-or-the-sewer-monsters-will-getcha feel.

By the time a brave passerby had shoved the lid back in place (trapping, he hoped, the underworld spirits for at least a little while), Dave and Sticky had descended the cold metal rungs of a ladder and were standing on the cement shore of a dark, lazy river.

"It smells *awful* in here!" Dave whispered (although, at this point, he could really have quit with the whispering).

"*Sí,*" Sticky replied.

"What are we *doing* down here?"

"Being superheroes?" Sticky said.

"We are not superheroes! We are . . . we are . . ."

"Invisible?"

"Yes! That's all!"

"But, *señor,* right now we should switch to Gecko Power."

"Why? So I can be the Gecko? What kind of crazy superhero is the Gecko? I don't want to be the Gecko!"

"Ay-ay-ay," Sticky said. "If people want to call you the Gecko, let them call you the Gecko." He eye-eye-eyed Dave. "There are worse fates, *señor.*"

"Never mind. Just tell me where I am and which way we're going. And what is that *smell?*"

Now, perhaps you've given some thought to what's beneath manhole covers as you walk across them or bump over them on your bike (or, for that matter, thump over them in a car).

Dave never had.

Manholes were manholes. Holes where men could work on . . . who knows what. He did not realize that beneath the street was a whole maze of channels and tunnels and corridors. That along the walls and ceiling of some of these corridors were pipes and cables and strange industrial boxes and grates.

He also did not realize that the dark, lazy river that ran through the maze was a collection of many things, but mostly water and waste.

So when Dave said, "Just tell me where I am and which way we're going," Sticky very calmly replied, "I think a light-stick would help, *señor*."

He scurried to a side pouch of Dave's backpack and hefted the small (but powerful) flashlight that Dave had learned to take everywhere. And when Dave clicked it on and took a look around, he said, "What in the world *is* this place?" He shined the light on the lazy river. "And what is *that?*"

"This is Sewer City, *señor*, and *that* is exactly what it smells like."

Dave looked at Sticky. "You're kidding, right?"

Sticky gave a little gecko shrug. "And unless you want to go through it, you should switch to Gecko Power."

Dave most definitely did *not* want to go through it, so he switched out the Invisibility in-got (being careful not to drop it into the inky, stinky river), then clicked in Wall-Walker.

"*Ándale, hombre!*" Sticky said, holding the flashlight like a headlight as he perched on Dave's shoulder. He pointed upstream. "Thataway!"

So, lickety-split, Dave scurried along the channels, moving like an oversized gecko with his hands and feet against the walls. He turned this way and that as Sticky commanded until, finally, he asked, "Are you sure you know where we're going?"

"*Sí, señor.*"

"*How* do you know where we're going?"

"We're following skid marks, *señor.*"

"*Skid* marks? What skid marks?"

"See? Right there!" Sticky said, flashing the light over a black gash on the wall. "You should see that *loco* honcho ricky-race around this place."

"Who? Damien Black?"

"You know any other *loco* honchos?"

"But . . . on what?"

"Oh, one of his get-there-quick machines."

Which was just the easiest way to describe Damien Black's Sewer Cruiser.

(Or, if you will, PU Cruiser.)

It was small like a moped, but with ape-hanger handlebars, and gadgets, mirrors, and gizmos galore. It was (of course) black, with a wicked rocket-fuel-injected motor that could go from zero to one-fifty in four point six seconds and wheels that turned sideways, transforming it into a sewage-spewing Jet Ski.

And as Dave geckoed his way along the walls, he began seeing more and more skid marks left behind by Damien's Sewer Cruiser. "We're getting close, aren't we?" he panted.

"*Sí, señor*," Sticky said, but his voice was small, and his little gecko heart was clacking like castanets.

"You okay?" Dave asked.

But just then they turned a corner, and Dave

saw a strange contraption glistening in the flooding light of a mega-watt bulb.

It had ape-hanger handlebars.

Gadgets, mirrors, and gizmos galore.

And it was parked, kickstand down, next to a narrow spiraling ladder that wound around a wide metal pole.

"We're here, aren't we?" Dave whispered as he came to a halt.

They were, indeed, there. And although they could have turned around and gone back the way they'd come (or could have found the nearest manhole cover and quickly escaped to fresh air and clear skies), the die had been cast. The momentum built. They'd traveled the entire distance from City Bank to the underbelly of Damien Black's mansion.

There simply was no going back.

Chapter 5
SNEAKY, CREEPY FOOTPRINTS

Damien Black's mansion looms like a monster high above the city on Raven Ridge. It's a house that seems held together by the unyielding forces of evil. With tall, pointy spires, shutters dangling from a single hinge, and odd, creaky, turning-pulling-cranking thingamajigs mounted in inexplicable places, the mansion appears to have a life, a *purpose*, of its own.

The mansion, however, is but the tip of the iceberg, as what is visible aboveground is a fraction of the vast heebie-jeebie creepiness concealed underground.

Deep beneath the floorboards of the mansion's first story are odd caverns.

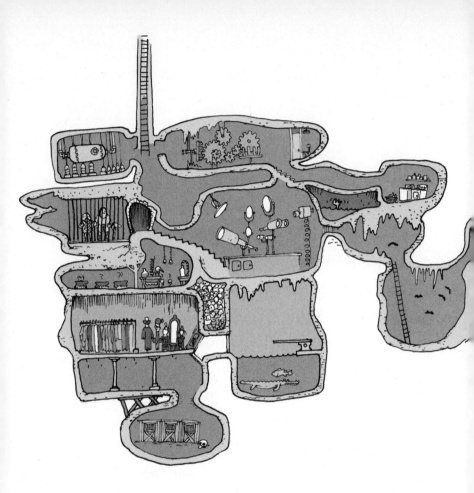

And caves.

And dark, diabolical dungeons.

There is also a massive den of dastardly disguises.

A mammoth chamber for sneaky-peeky surveillance doodads.

An enormous workshop that, besides the standard saws and hammers and wrenches, is chock-full of thingamajigs and thingamabobs, doohickeys and whatsits, and widgety-gadgety gizmos.

I could go on and on about the layered labyrinth beneath Damien Black's mansion, but for now, let's get back to Dave and Sticky, shall we? They are, after all, headed (in a roundabout way) straight into danger.

After ascending the narrow spiraling ladder for a few turns, Dave whispered, "I feel like I'm climbing up a big piece of rusty DNA."

"DNA?" Sticky asked, for he had, of course, never heard of deoxyribo-anything.

"Never mind," Dave said absently.

"Never mind? *Señor*, how can you say never mind?"

"Easy," Dave said, looking up, up, up the twisty, rusty ladder. "Like this: Ne-ver mind."

Sticky stood on his back legs and crossed his arms, staring at Dave as they continued up, up, up. "You think you're such a hotshot, *hombre*, knowing what this DNA is? Well, heeeere's a leeetle news flash: I know lots of things you don't." He got down on all fours. "Like, say, where we're going." He gave Dave a sneaky-peeky look and added, "But, then, that's something you're probably better off *not* knowing."

Dave stopped. "I know where we're going! We're going into the mansion. We're getting back Ms. Kulee's ring. And the bank's money. We're . . ." He squinted at Sticky. "What don't I know?"

Sticky squinted right back at him. "Tell me what DNA is."

"Oh, good grief." Dave started climbing the twisty, rusty ladder again. "It's deoxyribonucleic acid. There. Are you satisfied?"

"And what is dee-oxy . . . rybo . . . new-clay-ik acid?" Sticky asked, pronouncing it with careful respect. "It sounds dangerous, *señor*."

Dave heaved a sigh. "It's not *dangerous*. It's what you're made of. What *I'm* made of. It's like the blueprint inside of living things."

Sticky's eyes grew wide. "And it looks like a big, twisty, rusty ladder? Ay-ay-ay!"

"It's not big. It's tiny, in your cells. And it's not rusty! It's—"

"So it looks nothing like a big, twisty, rusty ladder?"

"Stickyyyyy!"

"What?"

Dave rolled his eyes. "Never mind."

"Never mind? How can you say never mind?"

It was at this point in their argument that they came upon a landing. It was simply a wide metal platform that led to a wide dirt path on the shadowy left and another wide dirt path on the shadowy right.

Dave hesitated at the landing, looking to the shadowy left, to the shadowy right, and then to the shadowy up-above (as the twisty, rusty ladder continued up, up, up).

At last, he asked Sticky the obvious question: "So? Which way should we go?"

Sticky leaned off Dave's shoulder, then ran, lickety-split, across Dave's back and leaned off the other shoulder. "Thataway," he said, pointing to the left.

"Why thataway?" Dave asked.

"Footprints," Sticky said. "Fresh ones."

Dave now saw that there were, indeed, fresh footprints leading to the left, away from the rusty

DNA ladder. "Where does that way go?" he whispered.

"Everywhere," Sticky whispered back, then shuddered and added, "They all lead to everywhere."

"Huh?"

"Never mind," the gecko said.

"Never mind? How can you say never mind?"

"Eeeeasy, *señor*." He gave a sneaky little gecko smile. "Like this: Ne-ver mind."

And so their argument started up again, only this time they kept one eye on the hard-heeled footsteps left by Damien Black.

The pathway was cold.

Convoluted.

And increasingly dark.

But ahead of them there eventually appeared a faint golden glow. Through Dave's mind flashed the notion that the glow could come from an enormous cavern of gold, but he tried to drive the thought away.

He was here to recover a ring.

And the bank's money.

Discovering a cavern of gold was not part of the mission.

Besides, a cavern of gold?

It was ridiculous.

Preposterous.

Totally and wholly unlikely.

Who but a madman would keep a cavern of gold in a place like this?

But, then again, Damien Black *was* a madman. . . .

The arguing ceased as they pressed onward because, despite his efforts to push the thoughts away, Dave's mind was now filled with visions of gold.

Until, that is, there was a piercing screech in the distance.

"What was that?" Dave whispered, his heart bending and twisting inside his chest.

"It might be wise," Sticky whispered, "to switch to Invisibility."

Again there was a screech. This time louder.

And longer.

And . . . screechier.

Dave's blood was suddenly running extra-twisty.

"Right," he said, and with a simple click-twist, twist-click, Dave removed the Wall-Walker ingot from the powerband and replaced it with Invisibility.

Immediately both Dave and Sticky disappeared.

Unfortunately for them, Dave's footprints did not.

Chapter 6
SCREECHES IN THE LIGHT

The blood-twisting screeching grew louder as Dave and Sticky crept along the pathway. "What *is* that?" Dave whispered again.

"Something eeeeeechy-screechy," Sticky whispered back.

"Do you think we're in danger?" Dave asked.

"We're always in danger, *señor*."

"But we're invisible!"

Invisible or not, Sticky was shivering on Dave's shoulder. "Whatever that is sounds verrrry mad."

"Maybe it's one of that madman's crazy recordings?"

This was, in fact, a possibility. Dave had delved

inside the underbelly of the mansion before and had been tricked into a state of extreme fear by a cheesy pre-recorded message.

Perhaps, he reasoned, what he was hearing was simply pre-recorded screeching.

Still, despite the fact that they were completely invisible (except for those pesky footprints), they sneaky-toed along, hugging the chilly wall, their eyes peeled back as if whatever was screeching might suddenly spot them and pounce.

The golden glow grew brighter.

Warmer.

And as they reached the turn that led to the glow, the screeching was suddenly silent.

"Ay-ay," Sticky whispered.

Now, "ay-ay" can, as I'm sure you've already determined, mean many different things. But in this particular instance, it meant, quite simply, Uh-oh.

"Shhh," Dave whispered (which meant in

this and, it's safe to say, *all* instances, Why do you always have to talk when we're in mortal danger? Why can't you just be quiet? What do I have to do? *Cork* you? If you say one more thing, I swear I'm going to leave you behind next time because you know what? You talk too much. Not only do you talk too much, you talk at the wrong time. Be quiet, why don't you! Just be quiet and don't—).

"*Señor?*"

"Shhh!"

"But why are we just standing here?"

"Shhh!"

A few moments later, they were *still* just standing there, so Sticky (quite understandably) whispered, "What are you? Petrified wood?"

"Shhhhhhh!" Dave whispered frantically. "Whatever *it* is *heard* you! Why else would it have stopped screeching?"

"Me?" Sticky said, pointing a little gecko finger at his little gecko chest.

"Shhhhhh!"

"Ay-ay," Sticky grumbled, and, as I'm sure you might imagine, this time it most definitely did *not* mean Uh-oh.

Dave stood there for another minute, maybe two.

His invisible back was against the wall.

His invisible eyes were cranked wide.

He was waiting.

Listening.

Imagining.

Sticky, you see, was right—Dave was, quite frankly, petrified. To be an all-knowing thirteen-year-old boy and suddenly not know anything (like what to do, or where you're going, or what that blood-twisting screeching was) would be, I'm sure you'll agree, entirely discombobulating.

And although the rest of him might have been stock-still, Dave's imagination was in overdrive. In his mind, he saw a heaping mountain of gold protected by a terrifying beast with sharp claws and long, oozy, needle-sharp teeth. A beast so vile and disgusting that a mere whiff of its sewer-laced breath could knock its prey out cold. A beast so mutated and ugly that—

"*Hombre!*" Sticky urged, pulling on Dave's invisible ear. "Let's mooooove!"

And so it was that Dave was forced to face the beast.

He took a deep breath.

He squared his invisible shoulders.

Then he stepped forward and came face to face with . . .

"A *monkey?*" Dave gasped.

It was, indeed, a monkey.

A small, moderately cute, but highly intelligent rhesus monkey that had been captured by

Damien Black on a treasure-hunting excursion in the Himalaya mountains of northern India, and was now kept (as was the case with all Damien's treasures) locked up tight.

But the cage that held this monkey was no ordinary barred rectangular enclosure. It was, in fact, quite elaborate.

Quite snazzy.

Quite *hip*.

The front wall *was* made of bars, but they'd been painted gold, as had the three interior walls. There were cushy couches, recessed lighting, and a full-service coffee bar—the cage was the mansion's subterranean espresso café.

It was the place Damien went to chill.

To unwind.

Or, more often, to get amped up with a stiff cup o' joe.

You see, the monkey was not caged simply as a pet. That beastly Damien Black had trained

him to brew rare and exotic blends of Himalayan coffee (which Damien enjoys drinking black, of course). Unfortunately for Damien, his prized, highly intelligent monkey had also developed a taste for exotic Himalayan coffee. (The result, no doubt, of being caged in an espresso café.)

Of course, as Dave approached the café, he knew none of this. He just saw a caged monkey in a gold room. A monkey who grew more and more agitated the closer they got, scampering from one side of the front wall to the other, pulling on the bars, stopping, whimpering, pulling some more.

"He knows we're here," Sticky whispered ever so quietly in Dave's ear.

Dave gave the gecko a questioning look.

"He smells us," Sticky whispered.

Which was true. Being invisible did not make them in-*smell*-ible.

Not that they stank—you and I would never have been able to smell them. But with an olfactory system twice as sensitive as ours, rhesus monkeys can smell things we cannot. And so it was Dave's odor, his natural (and appropriately managed) BO, that gave them away.

Perhaps you're wondering why Dave did not just continue on his quest for the stolen ring. He was, after all, in no danger from a caged rhesus monkey. Damien Black had obviously been and gone (as was evidenced by the still-moist espresso cup teetering on its saucer outside a small to-go window). And Damien's hard-heeled footprints were still visible, guiding them in the right direction.

So why didn't Dave just move along?

Get with the program.

Or, as Sticky would say, *ándale!*

It was the monkey. Something about his little fur-free face. Something about the way his eyes pleaded through the bars. Something about the whimper. They all said quite clearly what the monkey could not.

Set me free.

"Do it, *señor*," Sticky whispered, for he himself had been caged at one time by the evil treasure hunter and had great gecko sympathy for the little pleading monkey.

And so, after a quick glance around in all directions, Dave decided he would set the monkey free.

Ah, how unexpectedly dangerous good deeds can be.

Chapter 7
MONKEY BUSINESS

Opening the cage was, of course, not easy. There were nine locks dangling from each other,

linked together such that one could not be opened without the previous one being sprung.

And nine locks meant nine keys.

"The keys are here someplace, *señor*," Sticky whispered.

Which was quite logical. After all, if Damien Black carried around every key to every lock of every room in his nightmarish mansion (or its subterranean maze), he would be covered in skeleton keys (as they, of course, were the sort of key Damien Black preferred).

So Dave set about looking for the hiding place.

He checked the pathway for a trapdoor.

(Damien Black adores trapdoors.)

He checked the ridge above the doorframe.

(A foolish waste of time, as Damien Black would never hide keys in a place so clichéd.)

At last, he checked the wall. The bars, you see, were set back about three feet from the pathway. (Damien felt the recessed look helped give the café a more upscale feel. It was not, after all, supposed to look like a cage in a zoo.)

And although the wall seemed completely solid, Dave had learned from previous experience in Damien's maniacal mansion that he should expect the unexpected.

Keep his eyes peeled.

Be on the loony-eyed lookout.

Thinking like a madman helped.

And where would a madman hide a ring of skeleton keys?

(Think. Think like a madman.)

Dave began pressing the stones of the wall. They were cold and damp and rough, but he continued pressing them one by one until he discovered a stone that moved inward about an inch.

He held his breath and waited for something to happen.

Nothing did.

"Let go," Sticky whispered.

So Dave let go, and by doing so, he released the spring mechanism behind the stone.

A drawer shot forward.

A drawer that was decorated in great detail like an open coffin.

"Bwaa-ha-ha-ha-ha!" Damien's recorded voice laughed (for being the truly demented villain that he is, Damien found great humor in placing anything skeleton-related in a coffin).

Immediately a doll-sized version of Damien himself *boinged* into a sitting position in the satin-lined coffin and held out a ring of keys.

Dave had, of course, jumped back, and as he stared at the mini-villain in the mini-coffin, he whispered, "That guy is *wacko*!"

Sticky nodded. "One *loco caballero*." Then he added, "But *ándale*, okay? That doll is giving me the heebie-jeebies!"

So Dave grabbed the keys from the doll's outstretched hand and started unlatching the nine locks.

The monkey was, at first, simply confused. He smelled something, heard something, but did not see something. But when the coffin drawer sprang open, his little over-caffeinated monkey heart started *really* racing.

Somebody (who did not smell at all like Damien Black) was opening his cage!

The monkey bounded up and down the barred wall, swinging and screeching ecstatically as the locks popped open one by one. And when, at last, the final lock was off and the door was open, the monkey flew out of the café with a profound squeal of joy (one that only those who have known freedom and then lost it could truly understand).

"Good luck, little guy," Dave laughed as the monkey scrambled down the path in the direction that they'd come.

Then suddenly the monkey was back, charging past them in the opposite direction.

"No, no," Dave said, pointing an invisible arm in the direction of the twisty, rusty ladder. "Thataway!"

But the monkey kept right on going.

So Dave began refastening the padlocks (something he thought wise, as it would keep Damien

Black in the dark about how this espresso-café jailbreak had occurred). And he'd just finished clicking the ninth lock in place and was moving toward the mini-coffin when the monkey came scampering back.

This time, he slammed smack-dab into Dave's invisible (but very solid) leg.

"Wr-reeeeeeek!" the monkey cried, rubbing his forehead as he fell back onto the ground, dazed. But when he recovered, his nose sprang into action and a mischievous light came to his eyes. And while Dave put the keys back in the coffin and laid the Damien doll to rest, the monkey started slapping the air as he sniffed around.

"He's looking for you," Sticky whispered ever so quietly in Dave's ear (as he'd been keeping a watchful eye on the little rascal since the monkey had landed with a thump on his fuzzy orange rump).

"Huh?" Dave said, looking over his shoulder.

But he was already too late. That rascally rhesus was upon him now and made a solid slap against Dave's leg. Lickety-split, the monkey climbed his leg, then his back, and then perched on top of Dave's head, bending over to look him right in the eye.

"Wr-reeek!" the monkey cried, for he was now also invisible and could see quite clearly that the force that had freed him was, to his surprise, human. "Wr-reeek!" he cried again, this time bouncing with joy on top of Dave's head.

"Ay-ay-ay," Sticky grumbled, shoving the monkey's tail out of his face. "This is trouble, *señor*."

Ah, trouble indeed. For there is nothing, I promise you, *nothing* more persistent than a playful monkey revved up on coffee.

Dave took the monkey off his head and placed him on the ground.

The monkey climbed back on.

Dave took the monkey off.

The monkey climbed back on.

Dave took the monkey off.

The monkey climbed back on.

Dave took the . . . Well, you get the idea, I'm sure.

At last, Dave *tossed* the monkey (in an ever-so-gentle, be-kind-to-primates way, of course).

The monkey scampered back (in an oh-no-you-don't!-playful-primate way, as this had now become a very entertaining game of cat and mouse).

(Or, in this case, boy and monkey.)

"Switch to Gecko Power!" Sticky said at last. "Climb the walls! *Ándale, hombre*. This is crazy!"

And so Dave did.

Which caused the monkey to do a great deal of blinking and *eee-eeek*ing, but as Dave proceeded along the dimly lit corridor, the monkey simply followed on the path below.

"Eeee-eeek?" he asked. "Eeeee-eeeek?"

"Ay-ay," Sticky grumbled (which, in this case, meant How annoying does he want to be?).

"I feel sorry for him," Dave whispered.

"I think we should have left him caged," Sticky grumbled.

"What? How can you say that?"

"Not this again," Sticky groaned.

It soon became clear to Dave that the Wall-Walker ingot wasn't doing them an iota of good. They weren't escaping the monkey, and they were now visible (and, therefore, completely vulnerable should Damien happen back down the pathway). And to make matters worse, the monkey was terribly noisy with all his eeeking and squeaking.

"Can you just shush? Please, shhhh," he whispered, putting a finger to his lips.

The monkey pushed his lips forward, put a finger up, and whispered, "Whoooh" (which was as close to *shhh* as he could come).

"Whoa, dude, you're smart!" Dave whispered as he came down off the wall.

The monkey bobbed his head. "Eee-eeee-eeeeeeee!"

"Shhhh!"

"Whoooh!" the monkey replied with a finger at his lips.

"You're thinking dangerous thoughts, *señor*," Sticky said, for he could tell exactly what Dave was thinking. "That monkey is trouble. Big, big trouble."

But Dave, being an all-knowing thirteen-year-old boy (and having within reach something all thirteen-year-old boys want), did not heed the warning. "If you come with us," he whispered to the monkey, "you have to be completely quiet."

"Eeeek-schweeek!" the monkey replied.

Dave turned to Sticky. "I think he understands me!"

Sticky shook his head. "You're *loco*-berry burritos, man. I tell you—that monkey is trouble."

Dave grinned at the gecko. "So are you."

"Ay-ay-ay," Sticky groaned, slapping his little gecko forehead. But no amount of ay-aying, or ay-ay-aying, or ay-ay-ay-*a*ying would talk Dave out of it. His mind was made up. So with a simple click-twist, twist-click, Dave switched from Wall-Walker to Invisibility, all under the watchful eye of one rascally rhesus monkey.

Moments later, the three of them were proceeding along the pathway, the monkey on Dave's left shoulder, the gecko on Dave's right.

All invisible.

All heading, as I'm sure you've already guessed, straight for trouble.

Chapter 8
WHOOSHED AWAY

By straight, I do not mean in a straight line.

By straight, I mean directly.

Without sidetracking.

Or stopping to indulge in, say, after-school snacks.

The path itself, however, had nothing in common with a straight line.

It was twisty.

Jagged.

Complicated.

In long (as opposed to "in short," which clearly this is not), the path went up, down, in, out, this way, that way, pell-mell, roundabout, helter-skelter, and every which way but straight.

But it did, as you know, take them straight to danger.

"The footprints just stop," Dave said when they found themselves at a wide place in the pathway where Damien's hard-heeled footprints had, in fact, just stopped. "Where did he go?"

Ah, where indeed.

Cautiously, Dave stepped into Damien Black's final footprints.

Nothing happened.

He reached out to the wall on the right, stretching mightily to touch it (thinking that perhaps it would open some hidden passageway).

Nothing happened.

He reached out to the wall on the left, again stretching mightily to touch it (as Damien's lanky frame provided a much greater reach than young Dave's).

Nothing happened.

"Look up," Sticky whispered, pointing over-head.

Sure enough, there was a dangling pull chain. It was rather delicate-looking—like something you might see hanging from a ceiling fan.

Only it was longer.

And there was no ceiling fan.

Or any other mechanism, for that matter.

Just the dangling chain.

Up there.

Dangling.

Dave stared.

Sticky stared.

But the monkey (not being one for standing around staring) reached up and yanked.

Suddenly, *whooooosh*, a big, openmouthed Chinese New Year dragon dropped out of the ceiling and swallowed them whole.

"Holy guaca-tacaroleeeeee!" Sticky cried, holding on tight to Dave's invisible shirt as a

powerful vacuum sucked them up, up, up through an enormous hose.

"Eeeeeeeek!" the monkey cried, and the force of the vacuum was so great that the monkey (who had, unfortunately, failed to hold on tight to Dave's invisible shirt) was pulled right off of Dave's shoulder and (because he was considerably lighter than Dave) whooshed ahead of Dave and Sticky at an impressive speed.

Now, perhaps you feel as I do that flying monkeys are terribly frightening creatures. Regular monkeys are just fine. But flying monkeys? Oh my. They give me niggly-wiggly nightmares.

Flying monkeys are just . . . scary.

And (as you will soon see) I am not alone in this (admittedly irrational) fear—there are others who feel just as fearful of flying monkeys as I do.

Not that this particular monkey was an *actual* flying monkey. He was simply a monkey who, due to his own impatience and impulsiveness, happened to *be* flying. But he *appeared* to be a flying monkey, which is all it takes to strike terror through the hearts of those who get niggly-wiggly nightmares over flying monkeys.

And as fate would have it, there were three such hearts in the room where the vacuuming voyage ended. These hearts belonged to three men known as the Bandito Brothers: Pablo, Angelo, and Tito.

These three men were already in an extremely jumpy state because Damien Black was (understandably) furious with them. Damien had made it clear that he didn't want them around, didn't need them around, and didn't *like* them around. Yet during his recent incarceration (or, if you will, stint as jailbird), the Bandito Brothers had holed up in his mansion, making themselves quite at home, eating everything in sight (regardless of its questionable state or expiration date).

Damien had returned to find the cupboards bare and dirty dishes everywhere. He had immediately bound and gagged the Bandito Brothers and had begun plotting a way to rid himself of them for once and for all.

Obviously, getting rid of the Bandito Brothers required an especially deep, dark, diabolical deed, because Damien had paced around for three days, plotting, and had been uncharacteristically stumped as to what that deed might be.

And so (to curb his frustrations and replenish his dwindled cupboards and coffers) he had robbed a bank.

And snagged a ring.

It made him feel *so* much better.

He felt so good, in fact, that on the ride home on his Sewer Cruiser, he'd come up with a wonderful, fail-safe, deliciously devilish plan to at long last rid himself of those pesky Bandito Brothers.

"Bwaa-ha-ha-ha-ha!" he'd laughed while ascending the twisty, turny, rusty ladder. "Bwaa-ha-ha-ha-ha!" And after celebrating with a quick jolt of java at his espresso café and making a whooshing re-entry into the mansion, he'd passed by the Bandito Brothers with the sack of cash slung over his shoulder and pointed with his very pointy pointing finger. "Tonight, you fools," he hissed. "I get rid of you tonight!"

"No, Mr. Black! We are your friends!" Angelo said (although through the gag it sounded very much like "Oh, Mawa Bwa! Wa ah oh wen!").

"Ooo *nee* ah!" Pablo said, trying to convey the desperate "You need us" line that all double-crossing criminals use when pleading for their lives.

"You are *not* my friends, and I do *not* need you!" Damien snarled (for, much to his dismay, after three days of their gaggling, he'd learned to understand their tongue-tied words). "Tonight! I get rid of you tonight!"

Unfortunately for Damien, a flying monkey was about to make a nightmare of his deliciously devilish plan.

Chapter 9
FLYING MONKEYS

The Bandito Brothers, it's fair to say, idolized Damien Black.

They were in awe of his wickedness.

His deadly, diabolical dark side.

His sheer, unapologetic *badness*.

They had fantasies of becoming just like him. Anyone who had known the Bandito Brothers when they were petty criminals, stealing cash and curios from parties where they'd been hired to play as a mariachi band, would say that they were plenty bad enough (both morally and musically). But in truth, the Brothers were just bad boys in training.

Minor leaguers.

Damien Black, they immediately recognized, was the majors.

After they'd trekked a thousand miles to find him, they'd managed to convince Damien that they could help. They knew that Sticky could talk (something most people would scoff at rather than believe), and they'd convinced Damien that they could help capture the lizard and return it to him. "We have inside information about that sneaky beast," Pablo had said.

"Valuable information!" Angelo had confirmed.

"He eats crickets!" Tito had chimed in.

Now, it's a well-known fact that all geckos eat crickets. They love crickets. So this piece of information was not only not valuable, it was not helpful in any way.

Why, then, would Tito make such a comment? He was, in a word, simple. Slow.

Or, as Sticky often said, brainy like a burro.

But the Bandito Brothers did, in fact, know quite a lot about Sticky because Sticky had once *lived* with the Bandito Brothers. (Ah, the mistakes we make in our youth.)

At first, living with the Brothers had been fun, but it didn't take long for the Brothers to use Sticky's conveniently sticky fingers (and his undeniable attraction to all things glittery, twinkly, or just plain shiny) in their petty criminal escapades. These antics might have gone on much longer than they did had the Bandito Brothers not made a crucial (and predictably greedy) error:

They kept the spoils to themselves.

After all, what does a gecko want with shiny earrings?

Or diamonds?

Or cash, for that matter?

Like he could spend it?

This, then, was the attitude that drove Sticky

into the clutches of the devilishly deceptive Damien Black. But the treasure hunter was also not to be trusted, and Sticky soon found himself betrayed and, worse, caged.

Being a very clever kleptomaniacal lizard, however, Sticky had gotten his revenge. He had escaped not just with his life but also with the ancient Aztec wristband Dave now wore.

The one that allowed humans to become invisible.

Or walk on walls.

The one Damien Black would give anything to get back. (Not that he would give the anything up *permanently*. Oh, he would *pretend* to, but in his devious mind, he would devise some diabolical double cross.)

So Damien had grudgingly allowed the Bandito Brothers to stay, but so far, they had done nothing to help him get the gecko or the powerband back. They had, instead, contributed to his landing in jail and (adding insult to incarceration) had snooped through all his stuff and had eaten him out of house and home while he'd been away.

So this was it. Damien had had enough.

Those blasted bumbling banditos were history.

Yesterday's headache!

Tomorrow's daisies!

Gone!

Ah, but enter a flying monkey.

And what an entry that monkey made! The rhesus came whooshing out of the dragon-vacuum portal at an astounding speed, flailed in a wild, eeky-shrieky manner through the velvet curtain that separated the portal chamber from the adjacent room, flew clear *across* that adjacent room, and landed in a furry frenzy on top of Tito's head.

"Aaaaag!" cried Angelo (and even through the gag, it sounded quite like *Aaaaag!*). His scarred face contorted into a ghastly shape, and every hair on his arms (and the few he had remaining on his head) shot straight out.

"Aaaaag!" cried Pablo, his ratty face pinching in fear as his dirty, stinky pores shot BO in all directions.

"Aaaaag!" cried Tito, his oxlike body knocked nearly flat from the force of the flying monkey. (His head, not surprisingly, was unharmed, as it's difficult for a monkey to hurt a rock.)

"Eeeeek!" cried the monkey, for in all his adventures in the vast Himalaya mountains, he had never, I promise you, *ever* seen beasts so repulsive.

And while the Bandito Brothers aaaaag!ed in fear and the monkey eeeeek!ed in revulsion, Dave and Sticky (who had landed in the vacuum-portal chamber) peeked through the velvet curtain and, invisible as they were, were able to tippy-toe right past the lot of them.

"*Ay caramba!*" Sticky whispered when they were safely outside the room and moving swiftly down a cramped, cobwebby corridor. "Those *bobos* saguaros are still here? Why didn't they *vámonos* while that evil *hombre* was in jail?"

But Dave had bigger problems than the Bandito Brothers. He and Sticky had gone the only way possible, had passed by no doors, yet were now at a definite dead end.

Dave, who'd acquired at least some experience with the bizarre nature of Damien's mansion, took a deep breath and looked around.

The corridor had a planky wooden floor, so there were no telltale footprints to follow or stand in.

The ceiling had no dangling chains or visible escape hatches.

There were no levers or buttons or hidden whatsits or dosits on the cobwebby walls.

There wasn't even a picture (behind which a devious mind might *hide* levers or buttons or whatsits or dosits).

But what Dave *did* eventually notice was the *absence* of something. And its sheer missing-ness caused a gasp to escape Dave's lips.

"Look!" he whispered to Sticky as he pointed to the ceiling by the dead end. "There are no cobwebs up here or here . . . clear around to here!"

Sticky looked up, then tapped a little gecko finger to his little gecko chin. "Correctomundo . . . !"

"There's a whole half circle with no cobwebs!" Dave whispered.

"Which means . . ."

But before Sticky could finish his thought, Dave pushed hard on the right side of the dead-end wall. And before Dave could peek around and see what they might be getting into, *whoosh*, the wall spun around, sweeping them out of the cobwebby corridor and through the air, sending them flying into darkness.

Chapter 10
THE FIFTH DIMENSION—FEAR

"Holy hurling *habañeros!*" Sticky cried as they dropped down, down, down through the vast, eerie darkness. But just as Dave began thinking he'd spun through the Doorway of Death, he landed with a great *thump-bump-bump* on something rubbery-soft and began sliding.

They had, in fact, not passed through the Doorway of Death (although there were several such doorways in the mansion). Quite the opposite. This passageway, this *route*, was the one Damien took when he was in a grand mood. (It was also the one he took when he was in a foul mood, in hopes of cheering up.)

The whooshing doorway swept whoever pushed

it out onto a slide. A giant pitch-black inflato slide, with big air-filled bumpers on the sides, and swooshy twists and turns, all cloaked in complete darkness.

For Damien, the slide through the darkness was always over much too soon.

For Dave and Sticky, it lasted an eternity.

(The actual time was thirteen point seven seconds, which just goes to show that time is relative, especially when traveling through the fifth dimension—fear.)

At precisely thirteen seconds, Dave and Sticky went airborne for a second (well, for seven-tenths of a second, to be precise) and landed with a *flooop-bloop-whoop* onto small plastic orbs of air.

"A ball pit?" Dave asked, for he was, in fact, up to his neck in lightweight red plastic balls (although, being in total darkness, the color of the balls was relevant only to the demented mind of Damien Black). Dave waded forward. "*Now* what?"

This was a good question. A very good question, indeed. For every direction Dave waded led to a wall.

A dead end.

A no-way-out.

And while Dave waded, Sticky waited.

He rolled his eyes.

He shook his head.

He crossed his arms.

He sighed in the way only exasperated kleptomaniacal talking gecko lizards can sigh.

At last, he'd had enough.

"*Señor*. Are we going to wade around in a sea of balls all day? Or are you going to use the night-light?" (The night-light was not a little plug-in-the-wall doogoodie, but another one of Sticky's many words for flashlight.)

"I didn't want to give us away!" Dave whispered.

This was, in fact, a good thing to consider as,

although the flashlight itself was invisible in Dave's hand, the Invisibility ingot had no control over the actual beam of light. (Once again, the whys of Invisibility are not entirely understood. It appears to have something to do with the distance from the powerband and the conveyance of the wearer's body heat, but no matter. We'll just deal with the reality, and the reality was that the light beam was visible.)

After wading around in the vast sea of plastic balls for another few minutes, however, Dave decided that using the flashlight might be a good idea after all.

"Here, *hombre*," Sticky said, handing it over.

Dave shined it around and almost immediately discovered a ladder.

A tall, narrow ladder that led out of a swimming pool of balls.

Dave began climbing.

Up, up, up he climbed.

Up.

Up.

Up.

The ladder ended, at long last, on a long, bouncy platform.

"A diving board?" Dave whispered as he inched forward. He shined the light down at the sea of red balls (which looked to him like a sea of blood). He inched another foot forward.

And another.

"Not a good idea, *señor*," Sticky whispered, for the trip down looked to the little lizard like it would end in one nasty splat.

"I'm not going to dive!" Dave whispered. "What do you think I am, crazy?"

"So why are we out here?" Sticky asked, and he was now quivering, as Dave had inched out to the forward end of the diving board.

"Because there's got to be a way out of here!" Dave replied.

Above them, there was, indeed, a way out: a

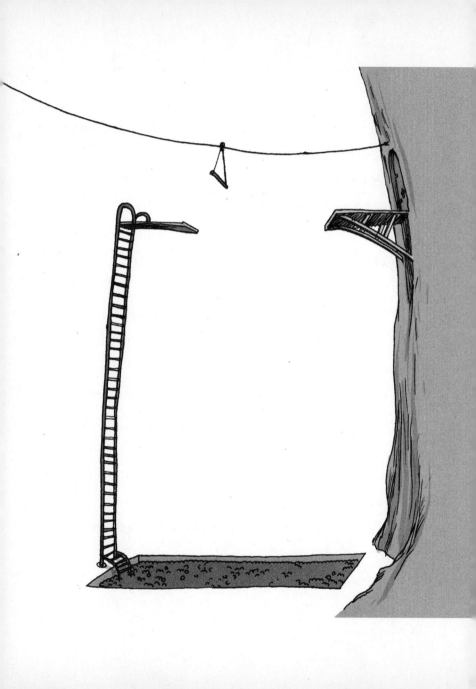

triangular trapeze bar that slid along a wire (by the power of a good push forward) to a seemingly solid platform by a blood-red door. All Dave had to do was *boing* up to the bar and swing over to the platform.

And if he missed?

Into the sea of blood he'd fall.

"Ready?" Dave whispered after he'd stared at the trapeze bar long enough to develop a kink in his neck.

"Uh, *señor?* Why swing like a monkey, or maybe die trying, when you could just switch to Gecko Power and climb the wall?"

Dave turned to Sticky and blinked.

Then he stared.

Then his eyebrows went all rumply.

Sticky shrugged. "Just a suggestion, *señor.*"

"What was I *thinking?*" Dave muttered, and, lickety-split, he switched ingots and climbed the wall to the doorway platform.

"See? Easy-sneezy," Sticky said with a very self-satisfied smirk. "Someday you'll start thinking like a gecko, *señor*. Then you'll *really* be the Gecko."

"I don't *want* to be the Gecko!" Dave snapped. "I want to be . . . I'm still thinking of a name. Invisibility Man, Disappearing Dude . . . something like that."

"Disappearing Dude?" Sticky's face twisted in disgust. "Why not just call yourself Lame-o Bandito?"

"Because I'm *not* a bandit!"

"But you *are* lame-o?"

"No! I just don't want to be the Gecko!"

Sticky shrugged. "Too bad, *hombre*, because that's what people call you." He eyed Dave. "And you should be proud. Gecko Power is *asombroso*!"

"Yeah?" Dave said as he put away the flashlight. "Well, I'm switching back to Invisibility right now because it's *asombroso*'er!"

After the switch was made, Dave squared his invisible shoulders.

He took a deep (and, yes, invisible) breath.

He faced the very visible blood-red door and said (a very audible), "Here goes nothing."

Then he boldly twisted the cold black door-knob and entered the mansion.

Chapter 11
RATTLING THE ALARM

Damien Black's security system was exactly what you might expect from a dangerously demented villain.

Patched together.

Complicated.

A haphazard hodgepodge.

It was, in fact, a messy web of amplifying, echoing tubes that Damien had woven together bit by bit as the mansion's size (both aboveground and below) had continued to expand.

Why echoing tubes and not, say, a regular ringy-dingy alarm?

Well, having an unfounded (or, if you will, un-*grounded*) fear of blackouts, Damien did not think it wise to rely on electricity. Instead, he'd rigged up the triggering of different sounds for each entrance to the mansion. One door activated a tinkly-winkly bell (which then tinkly-winkled throughout the house via the echoing tubes). Another door activated the string of a ukulele (which then ukulele'd through the entire mansion). The door that Dave and Sticky had just tippy-toed through activated a rattle.

Now, by rattle, I do not mean a baby's rattle.

Or the rattle produced by, say, a loose muffler bracket on the underbelly of an old jalopy.

No, by rattle, I mean *snake* rattle.

This particular rattle had been cut from an eight-foot sidewinder (which Damien had stalked and killed while on a snake safari in the Mojave Desert), and the spittery-spattery sound it made was fast and frightening.

Dave spun around quickly when he heard it, for although he was invisible, he was, in fact, quite solid and knew that snakes rattle when frightened and are masters at detecting odor.

He was, he feared, within both striking and smelling distance.

Sticky, however, pointed to the rattle (which was dangling in front of a flared receiving horn that fed into dozens of echoing tubes) and simply said, "That, *señor*, means trouble."

It did, indeed, mean trouble. Four rooms (and one convoluted corridor) away, Damien Black was completely absorbed in the counting of stolen cash when the alarm rattled. ". . . Four thousand six hundred and sixty. Four thousand six hundred and eighty. Four thousand *seven* hundred. Four thou—huh?" Damien's dark eyes darted about, a twenty-dollar bill poised mid-count. And since he was immersed in one of his three favorite occupations (tricketeering and gadgeting being the other two), he did not want to believe that he was hearing what he was, indeed, hearing.

But there it was, sounding like a long, rattly rainstick—the Snake Alarm. "Who the . . ."

Through Damien's mind flashed some hopeful possibilities.

A wayward bat?

(It was a distinct possibility.)

A runaway rat?

(Again, no stretch there.)

A menacing mouse?

(He was grasping for culprits with that one. Nothing so cute dared live anywhere near his nefarious mansion.)

And then a more serious possibility jumped into Damien's flashing mind.

Could the Bandito Brothers have rattled the alarm?

Had those buffoons managed to escape?

Impossible!

Unless . . .

Unless they'd been helped?

The twenty-dollar bill began to quiver in the treasure hunter's hand, and at last he laid it down with a bone-chilling thought.

Perhaps he had been followed.

But . . . by whom?

Agents from the bank?

The *police*?

They wouldn't dare!

(Or, at least, they had never dared before.)

Still. Damien Black did not like the idea.

Not one itsy-bitsy bit.

And although he still hoped for the possibility of a bat or a rat or a cutesy-wootsy mouse (that he could easily squish with his black-booted foot), in his devilish gut he knew something bigger was afoot.

Something irksome.

Troublesome.

And with the luck he'd been having, difficult to dispose of.

Why couldn't he just be left alone to count his robbings?

But the alarm had, indeed, alarmed him, so Damien scraped back his counting chair, snatched up his long double-edged axe (which had been leaning against a wall), and cautiously exited the counting room.

He saw nothing in the convoluted corridor (although the fact is, he couldn't see very far because, being convoluted, the corridor had only short lines of sight).

Zigzag he went, sneaky-toeing along his own corridor, eyes peeled, axe poised, moving swiftly in the direction of the blood-red door.

Simultaneously, Dave and Sticky rounded another corner, moving *away* from the blood-red door, and suddenly the two parties came face to (invisible) faces.

An interesting thing about being invisible is that you're never entirely sure that you are. There's a nagging doubt. A fear. A suspicion that something might not be working quite right. After all, you can see others; it's quite natural to worry that they can also see you.

Now, imagine for a moment that you've broken into someone else's house and that someone else is coming straight at you. He's tall, with cold, dark eyes drawn down into taut, tense slits, and his black, twisty mustache is twitching angrily under his long, pointy nose as he comes looking for an intruder.

You.

You would, I assure you, run.

And, I'm quite certain, scream.

So it was truly amazing that Sticky managed to choke back an *Ay caramba!*

And even more astonishing that Dave swiftly and silently sucked up to the wall, his heart *ka-boo-boo-boom*ing in his chest.

All the while Damien Black, a force of evil few would dare cross, bore down on them at a frightening speed.

Chapter 12
GERONIMO!

Damien Black whooshed toward Dave and Sticky, his long coat pouffed out with air and flapping at his sides. To Dave, he looked like an enormous angry raven swooping in for the kill.

There was nowhere to run, nowhere to hide. So Dave held another breath (on top of the one he was already holding) and closed his eyes (as some things are just too terrifying to watch). Then he simply stood there shivering and quivering and quaking in his shoes (because, let's face it, his nerves were shot).

In the wink of a deadly eye, Damien was upon them. But he whooshed right by, unaware of their presence.

Except.

Except that Damien's raven-winged coat caught on Dave as he passed him in the corridor.

Dave imagined that a blanket had been thrown over him (an easy mistake to make, as he was holding two breaths, had closed his eyes, and was shivering in his sneakers).

Damien said, "What the . . . ," but then dismissed the snag as being a pocket of particularly pouffy air.

And so while Dave held both breaths, Damien whooshed down the corridor until he got to the blood-red door.

He inspected the rattle.

The rafters.

The room.

He found no evidence of bats.

Or rats.

Or cutesy-wootsy squishable mice.

But he did *hear* something.

Something coming from the other side of the blood-red door.

Something . . . happy-sounding?

To a dark, demented mind, there is nothing more nerve-shattering than the sounds of someone else's happiness. Birds chirping, people singing, laughter . . . these are like long fingernails across an old, dusty chalkboard.

And to make matters worse, the sound Damien heard wasn't simply chirping or singing or laughter.

It wasn't just happy.

It was, Damien realized, *joyous.*

The treasure hunter cringed.

He quivered.

He covered his ears!

A great shudder moved from the top of his oily head to the tips of his ragged toenails as he gasped, "What is making that *sound?*"

At last, and with great bravery (for he was

truly frightened by the sound), he opened the blood-red door.

The sound became unbearable!

And someone had turned on the floodlight!

He stepped through the door, and what he saw astounded him.

Rendered him speechless.

Gave him a severe case of dropjaw.

In all his dastardly days, he had never, I promise you, *ever* seen such a sight.

Tito Bandito (the one who looked like an ox and had a head full of rocks) was bouncing on the edge of the diving-board platform, squealing with delight. Pablo and Angelo were in line behind him, and there was a monkey (*his* monkey) swinging from here to there, flipping around, eeking and squeaking, and having a golden time.

"GERONIMOOOOOO! WATCH OUT BE-LOW!" Tito cried, then *boinged* off the diving

board and cannonballed into the sea of red balls below.

Not one to remain dropjawed for long, Damien yanked in the trapeze bar and swooped down to the diving-board platform, landing with a great *whoosh-swoosh* of his raven-winged coat.

His eyes were like fiery coals.

His sneer like a razor of ice.

Angelo and Pablo cowered from the demonic sight, feeling both burned and chilled.

Neither had to say "Uh-oh."

They both knew.

They were in deep, diabolical doo-doo.

"What do you *idiots* think you are doing?" Damien seethed, moving toward the two Brothers.

"Having a little fun?" Angelo tried (for even a man with a scarred face and hairy arms likes to have a little fun—especially after having been tied up for three days).

"How could we resist?" Pablo asked. "It's the

ultimate playland, Mr. Black!" (And the Bandito Brothers would, in fact, know. They had been run out of many a fast-food playland and had never, trust me, *ever* seen one this remarkably radical.)

"Mr. Black! Mr. Black!" Tito squealed from below. "Jump! Jump! It'll make you happyyyyyyyy," he cried, flinging armloads of balls into the air.

"Shut up, you fool!" Damien barked at him. Then he came at Pablo and Angelo. "How did you get away? How did you unlock my monkey?"

"The m-m-monkey unlocked *us*," Angelo said, inching backward.

"W-w-we thought y-y-you sent him," Pablo added.

"He's a *flying* monkey," Tito shouted from below.

"You're a flying *idiot*," Damien shouted down at him. "Now get up here and catch my monkey!"

"Sure thing, Mr. Black, we'll catch him," Angelo said.

"We'll have him in no time!" Pablo agreed.

"Here, monkey-monkey-monkey!" Tito cried, climbing the ladder.

The monkey had, in fact, untied the Brothers. And being no idiot (after all, an idiot could never have unraveled twenty square knots, eleven grannies, five cat's-paws, nine half hitches, and three hangman's knots), the monkey now sensed that he was once again in danger of being caught and caged. So, knowing no other way out, he simply dropped from his hiding place under the diving board and scurried out of the ball pit and up the slide, back to the whooshing door.

"After him!" Damien cried, but while the Bandito Brothers fumbled and bumbled after the monkey, Damien himself took a trapdoor shortcut and headed straight for the espresso café. Something, he realized, didn't make sense.

If the Bandito Brothers hadn't let the monkey go, how had he gotten free?

Perhaps he had dug a way out?

Maybe he had over-amped on coffee and somehow King Konged the bars?

(Damien did, in fact, know that his monkey consumed too much coffee—*any* was too much at the import prices he'd been paying—but what could he do about it? He didn't want to have to make his own espresso, so a hyped-up monkey was simply part of having his own café.)

Damien, however, discovered no bent bars, no escape holes, and no sprung locks when he arrived at the café. Everything, it seemed, was perfectly in place.

But then he noticed something in the golden glow of café lighting.

Something sneaky.

Or, really, something *sneakerish*.

There were footprints.

Sneaker-toed footprints.

Everywhere.

Blood (what little there was) drained from Damien's face.

His body quivered.

It quaked.

Had an anger seismometer been attached to his temples, the needle would have shot off the scale, for it was at that moment that the great calculating mind of Damien Black finally figured it out.

"The boy!" he cried.

And with a great *whoosh-swoosh* of his black-raven coat, he stormed off to find him.

Chapter 13
ESCAPE FROM RAVEN RIDGE

It was all Damien Black knew about Dave—that he was a boy. He didn't know who he was, or how old he was, or that he lived with his mother and father and younger sister in a humble walk-up apartment on the poor side of town.

All he knew was that he was a boy.

A confounded, pesky, and maddeningly lucky boy.

Oh, wait.

That is not entirely true.

(The part about what Damien knew, that is.)

He also knew that the boy had a confounded, pesky, maddeningly talkative gecko named Sticky.

And that Sticky had given the boy his prized

magic wristband, along with the Wall-Walker and Invisibility ingots.

But really, *that's* all he knew.

Oh.

Wait again.

He *also* knew that the boy had dark hair.

And wore sneakers.

And sunglasses and a ball cap for a disguise.

(Which Damien found ludicrous, lazy, and ridiculously lame. He would have been right, too, except for the inconvenient fact that, being so generic, the disguise was very effective. Lots of boys wear ball caps and, when they're feeling the need to look cool, shades.)

But really, *that's* all he knew.

Except that the mere thought of the boy drove him mad (or, I should say, mad*der*), but that's really more about *him* than it is about the boy, isn't it? So I think this time we really have covered everything Damien knew about the boy.

What Damien was now piecing together, however, was that the boy must have released the monkey (as a decoy, no doubt), untied the Bandito Brothers (while invisible, thereby making it look like the monkey had done it), activated the rattle alarm, and been right there in the hallway when Damien's coat had snagged. (That last part, at least, he got right.)

As Damien stormed back to the counting room, he spat out curses and muttered things like "Drat that brat!" and "That pint-sized pest!" and "What *fool* thinks he can get away with this?"

"This" turned out to be much more than getting away with following Damien through the sewer system, setting free his hyped-up monkey, and infiltrating his mansion. "This" also included (to Damien's absolute fury) getting away with stealing stolen cash and a certain tiger-eye ring.

You see, while Damien was dealing with the Bandito Brothers and discovering sneakerish footprints around his espresso café, Dave and Sticky were discovering a table with stacks of cash alongside a tiger-eye ring.

"I can't believe it!" Dave whispered, and quickly shoved everything into the stretchy sack Damien had used to haul it from the bank. Then he made a speedy and invisible exit through, of all things, the mansion's front door.

And now, as he moved along the outskirts of the forbidding forest that surrounded the mansion, hurrying toward the property's large, tilting wrought-iron gate, he could barely believe his luck. "That was almost *too* easy," he whispered.

Sticky was perched on Dave's (still invisible) shoulder, facing backward. "No sign of him yet, *señor*, but I would *ándale*! He is going to be one steamed tamale when he sees what's missing!"

So Dave squeezed past the gate and hurried along the road that led away from Raven Ridge. But they'd gone less than a mile when Dave started complaining that he didn't feel well.

"Ay-ay," Sticky said. "Achy eyes? Squooshy stomach? Fierce bad headache?"

"Yes!" Dave said, looking at the gecko with surprise. "You feel sick, too?"

"I feel fine, *señor*."

"So . . . how do you know how *I* feel?"

Sticky gave a little gecko shrug. "That evil *hombre* used to get up-chucky when he went invisible for too long, too."

"Damien Black did?"

"How many evil *hombres* do you know?"

"So what do I do?"

"Take it out, or you'll be one pukey poncho."

"A pukey *poncho*?"

Sticky simply shrugged.

So Dave stopped, stuffed the sack of loot inside his backpack, took the Invisibility ingot out of the powerband, became instantly (and dangerously) visible, and continued down the mountain as fast as his feet could take him.

Night had fallen while they had been in (and under) the mansion, but the moon was bright, and as Dave hurried down the long, lonely road that wound away from Raven Ridge, he worried about being spotted by Damien Black. Perhaps Damien had boy-seeking missiles he could launch from the mansion.

Or hungry hounds he could unleash.

Or rabid bats that would flutter frantically around his head and bite him!

Damien Black was, after all, diabolically deranged.

Anything was possible.

But as Dave and Sticky finally crossed over the bridge that led into the city, no missiles screeched toward them, no hounds hunted them down, and no bats attacked with rabid fangs.

They were, it appeared, safe.

"Feeling better, *señor?*" Sticky asked as Dave hurried along city streets back to his bike (which, if you recall, he'd left near the bank).

And that's when Dave realized that he was, indeed, feeling better.

All better.

"Why does it make you sick?" he asked the gecko.

Sticky shrugged. "Because being Invisibility Man is not nearly as *asombroso* as being the Gecko."

Dave frowned at him. "That's no answer!"

"*Sí.* But that's because I have no answer, *señor.* How am I supposed to know? I'm a gecko. Maybe it messes with your DNA when you go invisible?"

"Your DNA?" Dave glanced at the gecko, shook his head, then said, "*Anyway*. Do the other ingots make you sick?"

"The other ingots? You mean the ones that evil *hombre* has?"

Damien did, indeed, hold all of the power ingots but two. He had powers like Super Strength and Super Speed and Flying . . . powers that Dave hoped to someday get his hands on.

(Especially Flying.)

"Yes, that's what I mean," Dave snapped. "Of course that's what I mean. Do all of them make you sick?"

Sticky studied the tips of his little gecko fingernails. "I only know what happened to that evil *hombre*, okay?"

"And?"

"And he only really used Invisibility and Flying."

"And?"

Sticky put his hand back on Dave's shoulder

and cocked his head. "And they both made him up-chucky if he used them too long."

"Great. Just great." Dave huffed, then turned to Sticky. "Why didn't you tell me this before?"

Sticky shrugged. "I didn't know it would happen to you. I thought maybe it was just that evil *hombre*."

"A warning would have been nice," Dave grumbled.

Sticky frowned at him. "Why are you being a grouchy gaucho? So you were sick. Now you're better, right?" He eyed him. "And just in case I have to point this out to you, *señor*, Gecko Power has never made you sick."

"I don't want to be the Gecko! I want to be Disappearing Dude or the Fantastic Flier! What kind of lame superhero is the Gecko?"

Sticky's face scowled to the left.

It scowled to the right.

He crossed his arms and studied Dave with a

scowl that eventually consumed his entire face. At last, he said, "You cut me to the quick, *señor*."

Dave tried apologizing, but Sticky (as you might imagine) was one ticked-off lizard.

But in the end, their fight might have been a good thing.

It kept Dave's mind off of the trouble he was going to be in for getting home so late.

And (more worrisome, even, than the wrath of a worried mother) the fact that Damien would, no doubt, come after him.

Chapter 14
TOPAZ ATTACKS

The first person Dave had to face when he returned home was not his worried mother. It was his saucy neighbor, Lily Espinoza. He accidentally bumped her with his bike as he entered the foyer (which was not so much an actual foyer as it was a dingy corridor with mailboxes on the wall).

"Freaky *frijoles*!" Sticky said, diving for cover inside Dave's sweatshirt. He wasn't afraid of Lily. It was Topaz, the sharp-clawed, ill-tempered, squooshy-faced cat cradled in Lily's arms that was the real problem. Topaz, you see, was obsessed with getting her claws into Sticky. (A condition caused, no doubt, by Sticky's sneaky habit of tormenting the cat.)

"Hey, delivery boy," Lily said in a mocking (and annoyingly superior) way.

"Hey," Dave replied, keeping his eyes down as he grabbed his bike and hoisted it onto his shoulder.

"Have a rough day *couriering* packages?" she asked, walking up the stairs behind Dave and his shouldered bike.

"Yeah," Dave said, wishing Lily would quit making fun of him.

Lily *was*, in fact, making fun of him. To her, Dave was a buttoned-up dork. He got good grades, did good deeds (like rescue her cat when Topaz was stranded outside on the apartment flower boxes, but never mind about that), wore a dorky red sweatshirt, and *couriered* packages.

Who couriers packages when they're in middle school?

Who actually uses the word "courier"?

Dorks, that's who.

(Which would, by her own definition, qualify Lily as a dork if it weren't for the fact that she wasn't actually *using* the word so much as using it to make fun of Dave.)

"Why's your backpack so stuffed?" she asked.

Now, Dave couldn't exactly tell her the truth (which was that it was stuffed with cash stolen from the bank), and since he wasn't very good at telling her to buzz off, he instead made up a reputation-supporting lie. "Uh, I checked out some books for Ms. DeWitt's project."

"Figures," she grumbled as they made the turn to the next flight up. "It's not due for two weeks, you know."

Dave nodded.

Topaz was really starting to squirm now, as Sticky (unseen by Lily) was slyly taunting her from his new location inside the back of Dave's collar.

"You carry all that weight all over town?" Lily asked.

Dave bounded up the steps as fast as he could (which wasn't all that fast, considering he was shouldering a bike and had a pack full of cash). "Look, it's just life, okay?"

"Don't I know it," she snorted. "All of us have burdens to bear, you know. It's not just you."

Dave, being thirteen, did not understand where this comment had come from, why she had made it, or how something so philosophical had come out of Lily Espinoza. All he really understood about Lily was that she was dangerous: gossipy, sarcastic, and nosy (not to mention unnervingly pretty).

By the time they reached the seventh floor, Dave was out of breath and ready to face his parents.

Anything to get away from Lily Espinoza.

But as Lily was moving toward her family's apartment, tossing "Have fun doing your *homework* this weekend" over her shoulder, Topaz squirmed free and shot down the hallway, up Dave's leg, and clawed her way over the top of his backpack.

"Ow! Ow!" Dave cried (in an admittedly dorky way, but, hey, cat claws *hurt*). He spun around trying to free himself of the cat (who was now hissing and clawing at his collar) and, in the process, whacked the wall with his bike, stumbled, and went crashing down to the floor.

"Topaz!" Lily cried. "Topaz, no!"

Now, it's a well-known fact that cats do not respond to the "No!" command. Even dogs in the heat of the hunt are loath to mind the word "no." It is simply instinct. The pursuit of prey.

So as you might imagine, commanding a sharp-clawed, ill-tempered, squooshy-faced fur ball to stop hunting down a smart-alecky reptile was completely futile. Topaz pawed and clawed and pounced and hissed, attacking poor Dave's head and neck and shoulders until, at last, Lily grabbed the cat by the scruff and unhooked her

front claws from their final, desperate clutch on
Dave's backpack.

"My cat *hates* you," she said, looking down on
the battered heap of Dave and his bike.

"Apology accepted," Dave grumbled, but before he could recover, he heard "Dave-y's in trouble, Dave-y's in trou-ble" singsonging out of his own apartment, followed by "He's home, Mom! He was out with his *girl*friend!"

Without a word, Lily disappeared inside her own apartment (as nothing makes a saucy girl take off faster than being mistaken for the girlfriend of a buttoned-up dork). And just as Lily's apartment door closed, Dave's flew fully open. (It had been cracked so that Evie, Dave's little sister, could keep an eye on the hallway and be the first to sound the alarm about her wayward brother.)

"Davey," Mrs. Sanchez cried. "Where have you been!"

"I told you he was fine," Mr. Sanchez said, looking down at Dave. "Rough day?"

Dave was untangling himself from his bike. "Very. Sorry I'm late."

"Dave-y was with Lil-y, Dave-y was with Lil-y."

"Shut up, Evie. I was not!" Dave snapped (as there's nothing like an annoying little sister to make a boy snap).

"You're bleeding!" Mrs. Sanchez gasped, and suddenly she was on her knees, inspecting his neck and the back of his head.

Dave simply said, "Topaz attacked" as he picked himself and his bike up off the floor.

"That cat!" Mrs. Sanchez huffed, and inside those two words were volumes of other words. Words like Why don't those people control that beast? And What kind of people let their cat tear up a boy and disappear? And They haven't heard the end of this!

Words that meant trouble between neighbors.

Trouble that could get as nasty as a clawing cat.

But for now, Dave rolled his bike inside the apartment and let his mother clean and disinfect his neck. And in truth, he was secretly glad Topaz had attacked. It had, after all, distracted his mother from asking questions about where he'd been.

So in the end, Dave lucked out.

Got off easy.

Hit the cat-scratch jackpot.

And as he drifted to sleep that night, he was able to put other things out of his mind and imagine ways of returning the bank's money and, of course, Ms. Kulee's ring.

How would he do that without giving himself away?

How would he let them know it was Damien Black who'd done the heist?

These were, I'm sure you'll agree, perfectly reasonable things for him to be imagining.

Especially since he could not begin to imagine what had followed him home.

Chapter 15
FOOTSTEPS IN THE NIGHT

Dave slept uneasily that night. He kept hearing sounds. Pittery-pattery sounds. Like footsteps, but not.

They didn't seem to come from the apartment above.

Or the apartment next door.

Or the *other* apartment next door.

It wasn't Evie doing another one of her pesky pranks (Dave checked, and she was fast asleep in the room next to his), and snoring was the only sound coming from his parents' room.

He stuck his head out a window to see if perhaps Topaz had escaped the Espinozas' kitchen window again and was bounding between the two apartments' hanging flower boxes. He looked high and low but saw no ill-tempered, squooshy-faced cat (which was, as you might imagine, something of a relief).

He also checked on Sticky (who was sacked out in his usual spot behind Dave's bookcase), but Sticky gave him a groggy "What's up, *hombre*?" to which Dave replied, "Nothing."

It wasn't until about four in the morning that Dave at last fell into a sound, glorious sleep.

Unfortunately, this sound, glorious sleep lasted only two hours.

At 6:07 a.m., an ear-splitting, heart-skipping scream rang through the apartment.

Dave shot out of bed, stumbling over his sneakers as he made for the door.

Sticky came flying across the room like a shot, grabbing on to Dave's hair for dear life, gasping, "What the *jalapeño* was that?"

"My mother!" Dave said.

"Ana! Are you all right?" Dave's father called as he ran across the apartment.

Suddenly they were all assembled in the kitchen (except for Evie, who was still, unbelievably, sacked out). And what they saw was something that Dave's parents would never, I promise you, *ever* have expected.

"There's a *monkey*," Mrs. Sanchez whispered, "making *coffee* in my *kitchen*."

There was, indeed, a monkey making coffee in her kitchen.

A monkey with a terrible headache.

One that needed a good, strong cup o' joe.

Now.

And it was a monkey with (as you might imagine) zero tolerance for anyone interfering with his coffee brewing (despite the fact that he was dealing with coffee that smelled decidedly inferior and a machine that was nowhere near as slick as the one he was used to).

"How on earth . . . ?" Dave's father asked, gaping as the hairy beast scurried across the counter, got water from the faucet, and poured it into the coffeemaker.

"Eeeek-reeeek," the monkey replied, baring his teeth in Mr. Sanchez's direction.

"Ay-ay-ay," Sticky said from his position on Dave's shoulder. (And in this case, "Ay-ay-ay" meant Hopping *habañeros*! I can't believe that fur ball followed us! We've gotta get *rid* of him!)

"What was that?" Mr. Sanchez asked. (And from the way his head snapped around to look at Dave, it seemed that he had *heard* Hopping *habañeros*! I can't believe that fur ball followed us! We've gotta get *rid* of him! instead of a simple "Ay-ay-ay.")

But the fact that he had heard anything at all meant that Sticky had, once again, slipped up. Dave was now left to rack his brains for a way to explain away the gecko's commentary.

"I said, I can't believe my eyes!" Dave said, relieved to have thought of something that sounded at least close to "Ay-ay-ay."

But his father's inquisition was not yet over.

"So you have nothing to do with this?" he asked suspiciously.

"Me? You think I brought home a monkey? Without asking?"

Mrs. Sanchez was shaking her head. "That monkey is making coffee, Ernesto. He's making *coffee*."

They all watched the monkey remove a coffee mug from the dish drainer and place it under the stream of hot (and very black) brew. When there was a drinkable amount in the cup, he took another mug from the drainer and, lickety-split, switched places. And then, with a great, happy *aaaaah* on his face, he gingerly sipped from the first.

Mr. Sanchez shook his head. "He must be somebody's pet."

"But he's making *coffee*," Dave's mother said. "And how did he get into *our* kitchen?"

The monkey kept one eye on the stream that

was filling the second mug and one on Dave's parents. When the second mug was half full, he put a third cup under the black, steamy stream and held out the second mug to Dave's father. "Eeeeeek!"

Mr. Sanchez just stood there.

"Eeeeeek!" he said again.

"Take it!" Dave's mother whispered.

At last, Mr. Sanchez stepped forward, took the mug, and sipped (all under the watchful eye of the monkey).

"There's a monkey in our kitchen making coffee," Dave's mother whispered again (as she was obviously still flabbergasted).

"*Strong* coffee," Dave's dad said between gritted teeth.

"He must've come in through the window," Mrs. Sanchez whispered.

"How? We're seven floors up!" Mr. Sanchez replied.

"He's a monkey!" she whispered. "They climb things!"

Dave's father turned a suspicious eye on his son. "But why *our* window?"

"I didn't let him in!" Dave said. "I swear. I didn't let him in!"

"What are we going to do?" Mrs. Sanchez asked.

"Keep him?" Dave asked hopefully.

"Are you *loco*-berry burritos?" Sticky whispered in his ear.

"Are you crazy?" Dave's father asked, then turned back to the monkey (who was already on his second cup of coffee). "I should probably call animal control."

"No!" Dave cried.

"*Sí!*" Sticky hissed in Dave's ear. "He is trouble, *señor*. Big, big trouble!"

Fortunately for Dave, a new presence in the kitchen caused Sticky's frantic whispering to go unnoticed.

"A monkeeeeeeeeey," Evie squealed, then charged past her parents and brother (and, of course, Sticky) toward the counter.

"No, *mi'ja*, no!" her mother cried.

But the monkey (who was, I'm sure you'll agree, no dummy) took one look at the little girl and realized real trouble had just entered the kitchen. "Eeeeeeeek!" he cried, then gave her his fiercest, hissiest look and scurried across the counter to the kitchen window.

And like a thief escaping into the night (although, yes, it was daylight), he hefted open the window, snatched his coffee mug, and swung out onto the flower box.

Chapter 16
CUCKOO

Dave Sanchez wasn't the only one who'd had a fitful night.

Damien Black hadn't slept a wink.

This was not because his prized Himalayan monkey had bitten him when he'd tried to recapture it and then made an eeeky-shrieky escape.

Oh no.

And it wasn't because those blasted Bandito Brothers had wormed their way out of a devilish demise and were, once again, eating everything in sight (as three days in ropes had given them quite an appetite).

It was the boy.

That pesky boy.

That tricky trespasser!

That infuriating infiltrator!

The nettling, meddling nuisance of a boy!

Into the night, Damien Black ground his grizzled teeth.

He sneered his snarly lip.

He paced the floorboards of his mansion.

From the counting room to the map room to the collections room he walked, stewing, brooding, scheming (and, yes, muttering about the boy).

What bothered him most was the thievery.

The boy had *stolen* from him!

Never mind that *he* had stolen the money (and the ring) from someone else.

That was irrelevant.

Immaterial.

In short, who cared?

(The bank did, of course, as did Ms. Kulee, but in Damien Black's dastardly mind, they didn't count.)

The pointy-point was that the boy had waltzed into his house and *stolen* from him.

How dare he steal his stolen money!

And so it was that Damien worked himself into a loathsome lather, entering the great room of his mansion shortly before midnight. He continued his pacing, first in front of the large stone fireplace (brimming with cold white ash), then in front of a hulking bookcase (three layers deep with tattered books). He then moved across the room and began pacing beneath a large cuckoo clock.

By cuckoo clock, I do not mean a cutesy-wootsy clock with forest-friend carvings around it and a little door where a tiny bird cuckoos each hour and half-hour.

Oh no.

By cuckoo clock, I mean something a little more cuckoo than that.

This one was made of black ironwood instead of walnut.

The weights running the clock were not brass pinecones.

They were cement-filled squirrel skulls.

The cuckoo bird's house was not trimmed with acorn-adorned wood carvings.

There were, instead, blackened bird bones.

And it was not a cuckoo bird that sang out each hour and half-hour.

It was a crudely carved cawing crow.

But as Damien's cuckoo clock tickety-tocked its way toward midnight (lowering the squirrel skulls slowly toward the floor), the gears in Damien's diabolical brain began turning at a frightening speed.

"Bwaa!" he hiccuped (for a wickedly delicious plan was bubbling up, causing him mini fits of laughter).

"Bwaa!" he hiccuped again, only this time, the clock began to strike midnight.

"*Caw!*"

"Bwaa-ha!"

"*Caw!*"

"Bwaa-ha-ha!"

"*Caw!*"

I should pause here for a small word of advice: You should never, and I mean *ever*, interrupt a deadly, diabolical villain when he begins bwaa-ha-ha'ing. It is both dangerous and dumb and will, in the end, get you killed.

Or, in this case, smashed beyond repair.

Damien's laughter sputtered to a halt. And as the crudely carved crow continued cawing, Damien ripped the clock off the wall and proceeded to crush it with his black-booted feet. Up and down he jumped, smashing, crashing, until, at last, the clock quit cawing.

"Bwaa!" Damien laughed, feeling better (and

quite in control, now that he'd quieted the crow). "Bwaa-ha!" And as the plan came back into his (no longer distracted) diabolical mind, a feeling of felonious glee blossomed inside him. "Bwaa-ha-ha-ha-ha!" he chortled. "Bwaa-ha-ha-ha-ha!"

This brought the Bandito Brothers running.

"You got a plan, boss?" Pablo asked.

"A plot to catch the boy?" Angelo said (for they had all heard Damien's mutterings).

"I wanna help! I wanna help!" Tito cried.

Damien gave them a dark, withering look, but the Bandito Brothers didn't wither. They instead tried to do the look themselves.

"Stop that, you fools!" Damien shouted, but his plan did, in fact, include the Brothers.

And what made it so wickedly delicious was that it would, he hoped, take care of two problems at once.

The Brothers.

And the boy.

Chapter 17
THE ELDORADO

If you were brave enough to tippy-toe past the wrought-iron fence of Damien's property and venture between his maniacal mansion (on the left) and the foreboding forest (on the right), you would do so on a wide, long-neglected path that was more mossy dirt than gravel.

And if you were brave enough to continue along that path and make it past the dual front doors (which are, I must tell you, thick white-washed oak, carved in the shape of a great, ghastly skull, with heavy brass clackers for eyes and a menacing mail drop for a mouth), you would round a corner and come upon a drawbridge.

The drawbridge extends across an enormous

hole (dug by Damien because he really, really, *really* wanted a place to put a drawbridge and didn't, at the time, have one). And if you were, indeed, brave enough to make it this far, you would almost certainly discover that the draw-bridge was drawn.

Now, by drawn, I do not mean drawn with a pencil, or colored in.

I also do not mean haggard, drained, or tired-looking.

By drawn, I mean upsy-daisied.

Horizontally neutralized.

Pointing toward Pluto.

In a word, *up*.

The drawbridge, you see, serves as both an exit ramp *and* a door.

The garage door.

Now, perhaps your garage is a hodgepodge of bikes and boxes and holiday doodads. Or maybe there's a drum kit and other band equipment keeping the cars out. Or perhaps it's stuffed with fishing gear or hiking packs or Jet Skis or (let's be frank, shall we?) a giant jumble of junk.

If this is the case, then your garage (and, for the record, mine) is nothing whatsoever like Damien Black's.

Damien Black's garage is there for one purpose and one purpose only.

The care and comfort of his 1959 Eldorado Biarritz.

Originally manufactured by Cadillac, the Eldorado was a long, sleek shark of a car with radical tail fins (designed to produce lift and thrust); broad, curving chrome molding (because, hey, it looked good); air suspension (for a smooth, velvety ride); and three two-barrel Rochester carburetors (because such a vehicle deserved more oomph than any conventional four-barrel jobbie could provide).

It also had, to Damien's delight, whitewall tires.

Damien (of course) customized the car to meet his unique (and decidedly sinister) specifications, until it was rigged and jigged and loaded with gizmos and gadgets that Cadillac would never (trust me, *ever*) have thought to provide.

Damien also painted it (in a moment of sheer frivolity) not black but the deepest, darkest purple imaginable and installed a fold-back ragtop to match.

The car became his pride and joy.

His coolest, most marvelous treasure.

His devilishly dandy delight.

It was, without question, his baby.

So it was with sentimental sadness that Damien now realized that it had been much too long since he'd driven the Eldorado.

His Sewer Cruiser had somehow usurped his Eldorado. Sure, the Cruiser was functional, fast, and *bad* (for a souped-up moped, anyway), and it did use very little gas (a definite plus), but it wasn't the Eldorado!

How had so much time gone by?

How had life become so tangled that he couldn't just take the Eldorado out for a spin once in a while? Top down, wind in his oily hair, white-wall tires purring on the open road . . . you know, just get out and *cruise*.

What doubly annoyed him was that he was thinking about the Eldorado now because he was saddled with those blasted Bandito Brothers. For his double-edged plan to work, he needed to get them into town.

Damien considered the possibilities:

It was too far for them to walk.

He couldn't trust them to get downtown on their bucktoothed burro (which was, in fact, the means by which they'd arrived at the mansion).

And they'd never all fit on the Sewer Cruiser. (Besides, he didn't want them knowing about his secret speedway under town—they already knew way too much.)

So after spending the night in his workshop (muttering and brooding and devising diabolical devices needed for his plan), he realized he had no choice.

They would take the Eldorado.

It would, after all, be worth it.

If they caught the boy.

Chapter 18
UNSIGHTLY DISGUISE

As you may recall, the Invisibility ingot does not make you inaudible (which is why it was important for Dave to be, *shhhh,* quiet when he was moving among people toward the manhole cover after the bank heist).

It also does not make you non-odiferous (which is why the monkey could smell Dave, even over the aroma of freshly ground Himalayan coffee).

And unfortunately, it does not make you disappear physically (which is why Damien's coat snagged as he whooshed by Dave in the convoluted corridor).

I say "unfortunately" because it was this solid

little fact that gave Damien Black his bwaa-ha-ha moment in the great room (interrupted as it was by the caw-caw clock). It was this solid little fact that had him working feverishly through the night in his workshop.

And in the end, it was this solid little fact that had him dig through his den of dastardly disguises and make the Bandito Brothers remove their absurd bandoliers and sombreros so they could, instead, dress up as blind men.

"I feel naked," Pablo complained, for although Damien had stripped them of their six-shooters when they'd arrived, they'd still been wearing their bandoliers of ammunition, and the weight across his chest had given Pablo a real sense of security.

"I feel bald," Angelo complained (which was, I assure you, more than just a feeling).

"Wheeeee!" Tito squealed, running around in circles with his arms spread wide. "I can fly!"

"Stop that, you fool!" Damien snapped. Then he took a deep, demented breath and hissed, "You said you wanted to be my . . . *assistants*." (Even saying the word caused him to shudder.)

"We do, Mr. Black! We do!" they all cried.

"Then you must *listen*."

"We will, Mr. Black! We will!"

"Shut up, you fools, and just listen!"

"We will, Mr. Black! We will!"

"DO IT NOW!"

The Bandito Brothers made big eyes and zipped their lips.

Damien took a deep, calming breath. "Here," he said, handing them each a pair of strange-looking goggles.

"Do these make us blind?" Tito asked cheerfully.

"The man said shut up!" Angelo and Pablo hissed at him.

Damien Black gave Angelo and Pablo a small, twisted smile. "Some of us are learning, I see."

Then he turned to Tito. "Quite the opposite. They make you see."

"When do we get to be blind?" Tito asked.

Damien pulled a villainous face at Pablo. "Can you make him SHUT UP?"

Pablo got his ratty face right up to Tito's. His eyes were like beady little coals of hatred. "We're going to *pretend* to be blind, you idiot! It's a *disguise*. Now, do you want to help, or do you want to stay here?"

Tito gulped and in a very small voice said, "I want to help."

"He'll be quiet, boss," Pablo said, feeling very much like Damien's right-hand man.

The treasure hunter glared at Tito for a solid minute before continuing. "The goggles," he said, strapping an extra-deluxe pair over his own oily head, "have one shaded lens and one *magic* lens."

"Magic?" the Bandito Brothers gasped, then hurried to strap on their own goggles.

"Yes, magic," the treasure hunter confirmed. "It allows you to see things that aren't there."

"Wow!" the three Brothers gasped, trying hard to grasp what this meant.

Now, the fact is, these goggles were not magic.

There was absolutely no hocus-pocus involved.

They were simply applied science.

Damien had constructed the goggles so that the right side was a lens like you might find in dark glasses and the left side was an infrared-detecting lens.

It could "see" heat.

The warmth of a body.

Any body.

Cow bodies.

People bodies.

Rat bodies.

And (let's get to the point, shall we?) invisible boy bodies.

Damien had very cleverly devised the glasses so that the wearer (by closing alternate eyes) could spot something that didn't seem to be there. (Had both the lenses been infrared, every person walking by would be visible, even the invisible—you wouldn't be able to tell one from the other. But by having one regular dark lens, the wearer could see both what was visible and what was invisible.)

This concept, as you might imagine, took a little while to convey to the Bandito Brothers, especially since nothing around them was invisible. But they did eventually get it, and when Damien had taken back the goggles (for safekeeping) and packed a supply of white-tipped canes and tin cups, he blindfolded the Brothers (which made Tito very happy) and then, in an effort to confuse them as to their where-abouts, led them round and round a circular corridor.

When Damien was at last satisfied that they were directionally impaired, he led the Brothers to a drafty-shafted elevator that lowered them from the mansion to the garage.

Once inside the garage, Damien removed the blindfolds and hissed, "If you so much as leave a fingerprint on it, you're dead."

"Oh, Mr. Black!" they gasped, taking in the deep, rich sheen of the Eldorado.

"It's . . . beautiful!" Angelo cried, and his arms went all goose-bumpy, shooting patches of two-inch hairs straight out.

"I've never seen anything like it!" Pablo said, his voice catching.

"Oooooh, shiny!" Tito cried.

The Brothers did another round of exclamations (because, honestly, they just couldn't contain themselves).

"Unbelievable!" Angelo gushed.

"In my wildest dreams, I couldn't have imagined such a car!" Pablo sighed.

"It's way better than a donkey!" Tito said with an approving nod.

Secretly pleased with their reaction, Damien slid behind the wheel.

He inserted the key.

He powered back the ragtop.

And with a mighty *va-vroom*, he fired up those ultra-bad Rochester carburetors.

The hungry growl of the Eldorado echoed around them.

The entire garage seemed alive with power.

"Get in, you bozos!" Damien shouted as he pressed the drawbridge's remote control.

And with that, they roared out the exit tunnel, across the drawbridge, and down Raven Ridge to the city below.

Chapter 19
TO THE BANK!

I'm sure you're wondering what happened over at the Sanchezes' apartment after their day was jump-started by a certain caffeine-craving monkey.

In short, not much.

Evie went back to bed, Mr. and Mrs. Sanchez sat around drinking (very strong) coffee, and Dave kept checking the window for signs of the rhesus.

"He's gone, Dave," Mr. Sanchez finally said. "And even if he weren't, you couldn't keep him."

Mr. Sanchez, of course, had no way of knowing that Dave was far more concerned about the monkey coming back than he was about keeping him.

After all, what if the monkey led Damien Black to the apartment?

What if Damien Black appeared at their door wielding his double-bladed axe?

What if he bwaa-ha-ha'd his way into the apartment and demanded the powerband?

Dave tried to calm himself with the thought that he could simply click in the Invisibility ingot and disappear, but another terrifying thought kept creeping into his mind.

What if Damien Black held his family hostage for the powerband?

He would, Dave feared, be willing to kill them to get it back.

In the end (as much as he hated to admit it), he decided that Sticky was right: the monkey was trouble.

Dave had other worries. For starters, he had a backpack crammed full of stolen stolen cash. He had to get it (and the ring) back to the bank (which, because it was Saturday, would be open from ten a.m. to two p.m.).

But his parents would (if this was anything like all the Saturdays that had come before) insist that he help with chores.

How would he ever get away?

As the minutes of the morning ticked away, Dave busied himself around the house. He swept the kitchen; washed, dried, and put away the dishes; cleaned fingerprints off the refrigerator

door; and wiped down counters (which had, not surprisingly, little monkey handprints on them).

"My," Dave's mother said after a while. "All this without being asked?"

Dave simply smiled and continued cleaning, keeping a watchful eye on the clock. It was already nine-thirty, and he had yet to come up with an excuse for leaving the apartment.

Think! he told himself. Think, think, think! (Which, of course, had the exact opposite effect.)

It was Evie who (unwittingly) came to his rescue.

"We're out of milk!" she whined from inside the refrigerator. "Mo-om! Dave drank all the mi-ilk!"

Dave had, in fact, not drunk the milk. There had been no milk to drink. But the instant Evie began whining, Dave said, "I'll go get some."

"Really, *mi'jo?*" his mother asked from the couch (where she was mending a split in a pair of Evie's pants). "That would be so nice."

So, lickety-split, Dave grabbed his bike, his backpack, and Sticky (who'd been enjoying a sizzly siesta out on the flower box) and escaped the apartment. He knew he'd be in trouble for taking too long to return with milk, but (being thirteen) he figured he'd figure that out later.

Right now he was focused on only one thing:

Getting to the bank.

Unfortunately for Dave, this was also Damien Black's sole focus. As Dave was speeding into town on his bike, Damien (along with the Bandito Brothers) was cruising to the exact same destination in his Eldorado.

Damien, you see, was banking on one thing:

The boy who'd stolen his stolen money was a doggone do-gooder who would return the money to the bank. (The fool!)

And (because of the magic wristband) the doggone do-gooder would want to stay anonymous.

And so (because he was a doggone do-gooder with a magic wristband who'd want to stay anonymous) he'd go invisible to return the money to the bank.

And he'd do it as soon as possible (because that's what doggone do-gooders with magic wristbands do).

So yes, there were, in fact, *four* things Damien was banking on, and it just so happens that he was right about all four.

Now, to Dave's credit, the thought of keeping the money (or any small portion of it, say one slim, crisp one-hundred-dollar bill that no one would *eeeeeever* miss) never even crossed his mind. He just wanted to get the money (and the ring) back to the rightful owners.

So as Dave hurried to the bank on his bike, the Blind Bandito Beggars arranged themselves (with, as you might imagine, much bickering) in various places near the bank.

Tito sat on the edge of a fountain (and immediately began fishing for pennies).

Pablo chose a place on the grass beside a DO NOT WALK ON GRASS sign (thinking how clever and convincingly blind he was).

Angelo settled on a bench near the base of the steps that led up to the bank.

TINKLE

And Damien.

Ah, Damien.

He treated himself to a double-shot espresso mocha latte supreme and found perfect outdoor seating at the coffee shop across the street.

Meanwhile, two blocks from the bank, Dave pulled into a quiet alcove, put on his hat and shades (just in case), clicked the Invisibility ingot into the wristband, and, *poof*, disappeared.

Then, feeling confident and determined, he set out on foot, heading (as you already know) right for Damien's diabolical trap.

Chapter 20
DAMIEN'S DIABOLICAL TRAP

Sticky was the first to notice the peculiar blind man sitting on a bench at the base of the bank steps. And although to Damien Black, the Brothers looked nothing like themselves, Sticky had lived with the Bandito Brothers and had seen Angelo without his bandoliers before. It didn't take the little gecko long to realize who the man really was.

"Uh, *señor*," he whispered in Dave's invisible ear. "We've got trouble."

"Huh?" Dave replied.

This was not the response "We've got trouble" deserved, but Dave was concentrating on piggybacking into the bank. There was an elderly woman nearly at the door, and he wanted to jet up the steps and swoosh in behind her.

"I *said*," Sticky whispered, "we've got trouble." Then, to avoid another "Huh?" he pulled on Dave's ear until Dave's head was facing the blind panhandler they were passing by. "That's Angelo!"

Dave had never seen the Bandito Brothers without their bandoliers or sombreros, so he did not believe that this was Angelo. "That's just some deranged hobo asking for money. See how he's talking to that paper bag? Now let go of my ear!"

Angelo was, indeed, talking to a paper bag.

It wasn't, however, just a paper bag.

Inside the paper bag was one of Damien's gidgety-gadgets: a walkie-talkie communicator. And as Dave and Sticky hurried to catch up to the elderly woman, the voice of Damien Black was hissing so hard inside the bag that the bag was pouffing up with very angry air. "There he is, you fool! Nab him! Nab him NOW!"

"Where, boss? I don't see him!"

"He's going up the steps! Right behind that old witch with the hat!"

"I don't see him!"

"WHICH EYE DO YOU HAVE OPEN?"

And that was the problem exactly. As they had been waiting, Angelo had done his best switching between his left eye and his right eye, but in the process of toggling back and forth, he had gotten tired, confused, and (finally) stuck.

When he switched eyes now, however, he saw Dave's infrared form (which, for the record, looked white, not red) hurrying up the bank steps. "There he is!" Angelo cheered, and immediately started after him.

The instant Angelo made his move, Tito and Pablo sprang into action (as was the plan). But Damien's voice (which was so angry it now crinkled the paper sack) stopped them. "IT'S TOO LATE, YOU FOOLS! Back to your posts! We'll get him on the way out!"

Damien was (as I'm sure is already obvious) furious. His deliciously diabolical (and double-crossing) plan was now partly foiled. He'd wanted to nab the boy, steal the stolen stolen cash, and get (at long last) the wristband back. Then he'd put the wristband on, disappear, and leave those Bandito bozos holding the boy (getting them arrested and deported and out of his life for good—bwaa-ha-ha).

But although, at first, the volatile villain was furious, he calmed down when he realized that the only thing he'd lost at this point was the cash.

There were, he told himself, plenty of banks.

What really mattered was the wristband.

If he had the wristband, he could walk into any bank (or jewelry store or 7-Eleven, for that matter) and take all the loot he needed.

Yes, he decided as he took a soothing sip of his

mocha latte supreme, getting his hands on this particular stash of cash was nothing compared to getting his hands on this particular wristband. He just had to wait and watch. And if worse came to worst and those bumbling Bandito bozos couldn't handle it, he'd nab the boy himself.

So while Damien regrouped (barking new commands at the Brothers through the communicator), Sticky tried to warn Dave that some Damien-driven plot was under way. "I swear to you, *hombre*, that's Angelo! That *loco* honcho is nearby, I guarantee!"

"Shh! We're invisible, okay? Even if they are here, they can't see us! We're safe."

Sticky, however, was sure they weren't. "*Señor*, there is something going on. Did you see those funkydoodle shades?"

"Sticky, shhhh!"

"And Angelo got up. Did you see that? He started after us."

"You're being paranoid, you know that? It wasn't Angelo. It was just some crazy hobo."

"Ay-ay-ay, why don't you listen?"

"Ay-ay-ay, why don't you be quiet?" Dave whispered frantically. "You're going to give us away!"

Dave whooshed into the bank behind the old lady and went directly to Ms. Kulee's office.

And Sticky *was* quiet.

For all of three seconds.

"Is there a back door to this place, *señor*? Because I think we need to find it and use it."

"No! There's not! Now *shhhh*!"

So Sticky shhhh!ed, but when he saw the note Dave left beside the sack of cash on Ms. Kulee's desk, he could no longer stay silent. "'Disappearing Dude at your service'?" he read aloud, his face scrunched completely around. "Are you *loco*-berry burritos? You'd rather be Disappearing Dude than the Gecko? Being the Gecko is cool, man! Being Disappearing Dude is lame-o insane-o!"

"Shhh," Dave said, zipping closed his backpack. "Come on. Let's get out of here."

"Disappearing Dude," Sticky grumbled, shaking his little gecko head. And knowing that he'd be wasting his breath to argue with or cajole a thirteen-year-old boy, Sticky decided to take matters into his own hands. As Dave headed out Ms. Kulee's office door, Sticky jumped off his shoulder and ran, lickety-split, back to Ms. Kulee's desk, where he crumpled up the note and tossed it in the trash.

And this, really, was all he was planning to do, but at the last minute, he saw the large ink pad on Ms. Kulee's desk, and this tickled his brilliant gecko brain into doing something more.

He opened the ink pad.

He did a quick flop-flop-flop across it.

Then he plopped the blackened bottom of his body smack-dab in the middle of Ms. Kulee's large desk calendar, leaving a nice gecko inkblot (plus a few scurrying-away gecko footprints).

After a quick foot-and-belly wipe with a Kleenex, he zipped across the bank, scurried up Dave's leg, and, *poof*, disappeared, catching a ride on Dave just before he reached the front door.

Dave was so intent on whooshing back out of the bank that he didn't even notice that Sticky had been gone. And Sticky, being so intent on setting the record straight, didn't notice that there were now *three* very familiar men (all wearing funky-doodle glasses) waiting at the *top* of the bank steps.

"Holy tacarole!" he gasped as they whooshed out of the bank.

Unfortunately, it was too late.

Chapter 21
SHOWDOWN

The Bandito Brothers pounced.

Dave let out a surprised "Aaaaagh!" but Pablo immediately slapped a hand over his mouth.

Sticky dived for cover inside Dave's shirt, certain that Tito (who'd been particularly fond of Sticky) would snatch him if he could.

To the rest of the world, it appeared as if three obviously deranged blind men (wearing what could only be described as funkydoodle glasses) were struggling with thin air.

"They're crazy," people whispered as the Bandito Brothers dragged Dave down the steps. And not wanting to be insensitive to the struggles of deranged blind men in funkydoodle glasses, people politely averted their eyes and simply went about their business.

"Excellent," hissed the paper sack. "Keep coming. Just keep coming!"

"It's that evil *hombre*," Sticky cried. "I told you!"

Dave, of course, now knew that Sticky had been right but couldn't exactly apologize with his mouth muzzled the way it was. (Besides, had he been able to speak, he would most certainly have shouted "HELP!" instead.)

"Sticky?" Tito whispered in glee. "Where are you, little buddy?"

"Forget that blasted backstabber!" Pablo commanded (sounding disturbingly like his demented idol). "Help us here! This kid is strong!"

Dave was, without a doubt, putting up quite a fight.

He kicked.

He elbowed.

He pulled and pushed and twisted.

But in the end, the Bandito Brothers overpowered him.

"You're almost there," hissed the paper sack as they approached the street. "Don't worry about traffic—it'll stop for you. You're blind men, remember?"

Had all this occurred with a *visible* thirteen-year-old boy, someone somewhere would have stopped the men in funkydoodle glasses. And it became clear to Sticky that biting Angelo in the neck, or shoving his tail in Pablo's ear, or tickling Tito into letting go would not save Dave.

But something else might.

Although it would, no doubt, make Dave mad.

But as the Brothers muscled Dave off the curb and into the street, Sticky realized he had no choice.

He scurried across Dave's chest.

Down his arm!

To the wristband!

And, using the awesome grip of his gecko hands, did a quick click-twist and removed the Invisibility ingot.

POOF! Dave appeared.

"HELP!" Sticky shouted at the top of his (surprisingly powerful) gecko lungs. And since he was still inside Dave's sweatshirt, it sounded for all the world like the cry was coming from Dave.

Across the street, Damien jumped to his dastardly feet and moved toward Dave.

Traffic slowed, then stopped.

And Damien might simply have charged the boy, snatched the powerband, and escaped if two things had not occurred nearly simultaneously.

First, the first thing:

Pablo and Tito (having, presumably, switched eyes a few times) had released their hold on Dave, but Angelo was not about to let go until his boss ordered him to. So Sticky, realizing that Angelo was all that was standing between Dave and his escape, bit Angelo's hand.

Hard.

Unfortunately, the bite made Angelo's hand jerk so hard that he knocked poor Sticky, not just off of Dave and onto the street, but *out*.

The poor little lizard never even saw stars.

No twittering tweety birds.

He just blacked out.

As Sticky was being knocked out, his amazingly sticky fingers released the Invisibility ingot, which went flying in the opposite direction, then rolled in a little circle before clinking to a very shiny stop on the ground.

Suddenly everything in the street went still as Damien faced off with Dave.

This was, without question, a showdown.

Three paces to the left was a talking (although presently unconscious) kleptomaniacal gecko lizard.

Three paces to the right was the magic ingot of any boy's dreams.

The Bandito Brothers might have helped Damien, but Damien didn't trust them not to bungle the whole situation. "Back off," he growled at them. "Don't move a muscle."

Damien's dark, glinting eyes watched for Dave (still wearing his dark, not-so-glinting glasses) to make a move. And in the treasure hunter's dark, devilish heart, he knew that the boy could not resist the ingot.

What boy could?

Damien's face sneered into a silent bwaa-ha-ha, for the instant Dave moved toward the ingot, he would pounce on him, rip the powerband off, click in the ingot, and disappear.

This face-to-face showdown appeared to be in slow motion, but in reality, it lasted only a few seconds before the *second* thing happened.

The second thing being, someone shouted.

And it wasn't just that they shouted.

It was *what* they shouted.

"Stop that monkey!"

Out of the coffee shop charged a rhesus, a to-go cup of coffee in one hand, a vacuum pack of premium-blend beans in the other.

"Eeeeeek," he cried, skidding to a halt at the sobering sight of Damien Black. "Eeek-creeeeek?" he said, taking in Dave and the funkydoodled Bandito Brothers.

Dave jolted toward the ingot.

Damien lunged for it.

But Dave had only faked a move in that direction, and with Damien now going the wrong way, Dave went the other, scooped up Sticky, and did what any kid without the power to disappear would do.

He *ran*.

Chapter 22
THE GREATEST POWER OF ALL

Dave did not see what happened after he made his escape.

He did not see the monkey fly at Damien as the villain was lunging for the ingot.

He did not see the monkey rip at Damien's oily black hair and pounce up and down on his head.

He did not see the monkey scramble all over him, causing Damien to spin in circles and cry, "Stop him, you fools! Get him off of me!"

And he did not, I'm most sorry to report, see that hyped-up monkey pour what was left of the to-go coffee all over Damien's head.

No, for all Dave knew, Damien Black had

snapped up the ingot and was chasing after him for the powerband.

So Dave was worried.

Very worried.

But he was most worried about Sticky.

He couldn't really tell . . . was Sticky dead?

Dave's heart was pounding and breaking at the same time as he snatched up his bike and ped-aled home. He held the handlebars with one hand and Sticky with the other, blinking back tears as he talked to the lizard. "I'm so sorry!" he choked out. "I should have listened! Please wake up. Please be all right. Sticky? Sticky, can you hear me? You saved my life, you know that? I couldn't have gotten away from them without you." His eyes welled as he pedaled harder. "What have I done!"

The whole trip home, Dave talked.

The whole trip home, he begged Sticky to wake up.

The whole trip home, Sticky just lay there, still.

Until, that is, they rounded the corner onto Dave's street. "You can zip it now," the little gecko groaned. "I'm awake."

"STICKY!" Dave cried, skidding to a halt.

"Shhh!" Sticky said, holding his head. "Ay-ay-ay. That was one bad bonk." He looked at Dave. "What happened, *señor*? Last I remember, I was taking a big juicy chomp of Angelo's hand."

So Dave told him what had happened, and when he was done, Sticky was up on all fours, looking at him with his head cocked.

"Why are you staring at me like that?" Dave asked.

Sticky looked at him another moment, then simply shook his head. He was, for once, at a loss for words. And no "Ay-ay-ay" could begin to convey what he was feeling.

So I will do my best to translate:

What makes a real superhero is not the powers they have, it's the way they choose to use those powers.

Dave had chosen Sticky *over* power.

(And, anyone would agree, a really *super* power at that.)

How could the little gecko explain that no matter what he wanted to call himself, Dave was, indeed, a superhero and that in his heart he held the greatest power of all.

Well, he simply couldn't.

So he did the next best thing:

He got on Dave's shoulder.

When they were at last in front of their walk-up, he said, "Hey, *hombre*, aren't you supposed to be bringing home some milk?"

"Oh!" Dave said, doing a quick U-turn. "Right!"

Unfortunately for Dave, his parents didn't exactly buy the story about his pet lizard falling off his shoulder and rushing downtown to try to find a reptile veterinarian. His mother wagged a finger at him and scolded, "You tell us you're going to get some milk, then you disappear for an hour and expect us to buy some wild story about your lizard getting hurt?"

Sticky drooped like he was sick and gave her a look that conveyed complete and utter agony.

Dave's mother sized him up. "He looks fine to me."

"But it's true, Mom!"

"Dave-y's got a girlfriend, Dave-y's got a girl-friend!"

"Shut up, Evie!"

"You shut up!"

"If you have a girlfriend, just tell us," his dad grumbled. "Is it the girl next door?"

"No!"

"Then who? Tell us, or you're grounded."

"Dad! I don't have a girlfriend!"

"Dave-y's lying, Dave-y's lying!"

"Ay-ay-ay," Sticky grumbled, covering his ears.

"What was that?" Mr. Sanchez asked.

"I'm not lying!" Dave said, doing his best to cover up for Sticky.

"Just stop with the disappearing act, okay, mi'jo?" his mother said.

With a heavy heart, Dave agreed. "Not a problem," he said, thinking that his disappearing days were, indeed, over.

Ah, but how could he predict what the future would hold?

He couldn't. And it's a future that I would happily tell you all about, but, really, it's a story for another time, another place, and . . .

Oh, all right. I suppose I could tell you a few more things. . . .

Like that Dave ran into a very excited Lily Espinoza on the stairs later that day. "He's back!" she cried. "The Gecko's back!"

"What?" Dave asked.

"It was on the news! He stopped a bank heist!"

"Wait a minute," Dave said, and he (very uncharacteristically) grabbed her arm. "Who says it was the Gecko?"

"They showed his sign. His signature! It's amazing! *He's* amazing." She broke away, saying, "Gotta go, bye!" and raced down the stairs.

I could also, I suppose, tell you that since nobody could figure out what the ruckus in the street was about, Damien Black simply drove his Eldorado back up to Raven Ridge.

Alone.

And that the Bandito Brothers, being no strangers to walking, set off on the long trek back to the mansion to help their boss recover from his traumatic ordeal. (And that, as you might imagine, Damien was less than overjoyed to find them clacking the eyes of his skull door and yelling, "Boss, we're home!" through the mail slot.)

I could *also* tell you that a certain caffeine-crazed monkey did return to the Sanchezes' apartment a few days later (this time, with his own supply of premium blend) and that he slipped a hard metal object into the bottom of the cup he served to Dave.

A key.

A key that was strange in both shape and color.

A key that went to . . . Dave had no idea.

However, when *Sticky* saw it, he . . .

Ah, but I really must stop. As I said, these are stories for another time, another place.

For now, the money is back at the bank, as it should be.

For now, the ring is back on Ms. Kulee's finger, where it belongs.

And so, my friend, for today, the time has come to say . . .

Adiós!

A GUIDE TO SPANISH AND STICKYNESE TERMS

adiós (Spanish / *ah-DEE-ohs*): goodbye, see ya later, alligator

ándale (Spanish / *AHN-duh-lay*): hurry up! come on! get a move on!

asombroso (Spanish / *ah-sohm-BRO-so*): awesome, amazing

ay-ay-ay (Spanish and a Sticky favorite): depending on the
inflection, this could mean oh brother, oh please, or you
have *got* to be kidding!

ay caramba (Spanish and a Sticky favorite / *ai cah-RAHM-bah*): oh
wow! or oh brother! or I am not believing this!

bobo (Spanish / *BO-bo*): dumb, foolish, silly

bobos banditos (Stickynese / *BO-bohs bahn-DEE-tohs*): crazy ban-
dits, stupid thieves

caballero (Spanish / *cah-buhl-YAIR-oh*): gentleman, knight, nobleman

creeping creosote (Stickynese / *CREE-uh-soht*): literally, oozing,
thick, oily stuff derived from coal. But in Stickynese, holy
smokes!

easy-sneezy (Stickynese): piece of cake, no sweat

freaky *frijoles* (Stickynese / *free-HO-lays*): literally, weird beans.
But for Sticky, oh wow! or how strange!

gaucho (Spanish / *GOW-cho*): herdsman, cowboy

holy guaca-tacarole (Stickynese / gwah-cuh-*tah-cuh-RO-lee*): holy
smokes!

hombre (Spanish / *AHM-bray*): man, dude

hopping / hurling *habañeros* (Stickynese / *ah-bahn-YAIR-ohs*): literally, hopping hot peppers. But for Sticky, oh my gosh!

loco (Spanish / *LO-co*): crazy, loony

loco-**berry burritos** (Stickynese): literally, crazy-berry rolled tor-
tillas. But for Sticky, extra-specially crazy

mi'ja (Spanish / *MEE-ha*): dear, darling, my daughter, my love.
For a boy, you'd say *mi'jo* (*MEE-ho*)

señor (Spanish / *SEN-yohr*): mister

sí (Spanish / *see*): yes

vámonos (Spanish / VAH-mo-nohs): let's go!